THE

FREEBORN

SLAVES.

By

TONY ODOH.

The Freeborn Slaves.

Copyright.

Published by;

© 2023 BY TONY IK ODOH

All rights reserved. No part of this publication may be reproduced, stored, distributed, or transmitted in any form or by any means, including photocopying, recording, or other electronic or mechanical methods, without the prior written permission of the publisher, except in the case of brief quotations embodied in critical reviews and certain other noncommercial uses permitted by copyright law.

Warning!

This book is a work of fiction. The information, circumstances, and opinions presented herein are based on the author's imagination and personal experiences. The author makes no representations or warranties of any kind, express or implied, about the completeness, accuracy, reliability, suitability, or availability of the information contained in this book. The story here is not real and does not depict or connote any event, culture, or people anywhere. Any resemblance is a mere coincidence.

Cover design by Tony Odoh.

The Freeborn Slaves.

Table of Contents

THE FREEBORN SLAVES. 1

Copyright. 2

Dedication. 6

Appreciation. 7

Synopsis. 8

Chapter 1 11

Chapter 2 19

Chapter 3 23

Chapter 4 29

Chapter 5 35

Chapter 6 39

Chapter 7 45

Chapter 8 49

Chapter 9 51

Chapter 10 65

Chapter 11. 73

Chapter 12. 79

Chapter 13. 81

Chapter 14. 87

Chapter 15. 91

Chapter 16. 95

The Freeborn Slaves.

Chapter 17. 97
Chapter 18. 99
Chapter 19. 105
Chapter 20. 107
Chapter 21. 111
Chapter 22. 117
Chapter 23. 123
Chapter 24. 135
Chapter 25. 139
Chapter 26. 145
Chapter 27. 151
Chapter 28. 157
Chapter 29. 169
Chapter 30. 173
Chapter 31. 177
Chapter 32. 181
Chapter 33. 193
Chapter 34. 199
Chapter 35. 201
Chapter 36. 207
Chapter 37. 211
Chapter 38. 213
Chapter 39. 223

The Freeborn Slaves.

Chapter 40. 225

Chapter 41. 229

Chapter 42. 243

Chapter 43. 251

Chapter 44. 255

Chapter 45. 263

Chapter 46. 273

Chapter 47. 286

Chapter 48. 288

Dedication.

This book is dedicated to all people who suffer discrimination, segregation, and deprivation as a result of circumstances beyond their control.

The Freeborn Slaves.

Appreciation.

In sincere gratitude, I appreciate my wife Oge, and my children for sparing me the time to write this story. I appreciate my brothers and sisters. I appreciate Deman and Uche Nobert who gingered me to take up story writing.

The Freeborn Slaves.

Synopsis.

The "Osu" caste system is a traditional social hierarchy found among the Igbo people in Nigeria, particularly in the southeastern region known as Igboland. The term "Osu" refers to individuals or families historically deemed as "outcasts" or "untouchables" within the Igbo society. This caste system is deeply rooted in ancient Igbo beliefs and practices, where certain individuals or families were segregated and considered spiritually polluted due to perceived offenses or circumstances. The reasons for being designated as an "Osu" vary, including engaging in activities deemed taboo or being descendants of slaves. Over time, efforts have been made to challenge and abolish this discriminatory system, as it is considered unjust and inconsistent with modern principles of equality and human rights. Various Igbo communities have taken steps to eliminate the stigma associated with the "Osu" caste system, advocating for equal treatment and opportunities for all members of society.
Thus the book "The Freeborn Slaves: A Fight For Freedom" is an attempt to criticize and correct this anomaly and injustice.

....

In the village of Owere, the "Osu" caste system caused discrimination, deprivation, and severe inhumane treatment for some people in the village. The suffering was unbearable, to the point that the "Osu" were not allowed to go to the river or even see the "sacred" carnivals of the revered village

The Freeborn Slaves.

masquerades and their followers performing during the festivities because they consider the eyes of the "Osu" unclean, and unworthy to see sacred things. From using service and charity to applying violence for violence, to using what they call peaceful violence, one family endured severe personal losses for three generations fighting to liberate the village's "Osu" faction and unite the two sides.

The Freeborn Slaves.

The Freeborn Slaves.

Chapter 1

The morning promises to be an interesting one more than usual. BigChild was on his routine visit to La Medina Resort, one of the numerous businesses built by his father, Pa Lui, The Don. A few moments after settling down to peruse one of the resumes, Everestus, the manager, came to report that Ijeuwa, a Booty-for-all girl had refused to finish her job. And what's her job you may ask, but that is the story for another day. The name Booty-for-all is after all a corruption of the word "beautiful" girls of the Resort. However, for members of the club, it is a corrupted way of calling the carefully selected pretty girls of the club.

"I'm not doing anything again!" Ijeuwa vehemently insisted on ignoring the presence of her boss BigChild.

"God, where are you?" She queried the space before her, tears of agony flowing down her face. "How could you create me and abandon me? Forgotten?" She continued to cry and insisted that she would rather die than continue with the servicing job. In her twenty-something years on earth, she had suffered more than her share for ten lifetimes.

BigChild was more than dumbfounded- he was lost in mental puzzles. In his entire life, he had never seen anyone dare him to his face like this let alone his staff. Now, he has not just been dared but he is not even infuriated or feeling so insulted as he expected of himself.

The Freeborn Slaves.

"What's she talking about?" BigChild heard himself asking nobody in particular- he was confused. On his good day, the Big Child would not tolerate such insolence and insubordination. He would order his subordinates to teach her the bitter lesson of her life for her rude utterances. He has the money; the clout and the guts, and he has the arrogance too. After all, his father was The Don- the dreaded mean man and he himself is no less mean, but this time, he didn't know why he kept his cool. Does this unusual coolness have something to do with the document that he retrieved from the registry? He wondered. Maybe not but he really didn't know.

"And why are you looking at me like that?!" Ijeuwa shouted at BigChild as if to spill petrol onto a raging fire. "As a matter of fact," she went on, "kill me now and end it all. I've been to hell and back as hell too refused to even touch, let alone consume me." She had exploded by then and tears of sorrow walked down her cheeks. She sat on the floor of the room be-moaning her life. BigChild had left her then. She was watching with her mind's eye as the memories she wished to forget about her life replayed.

Soon BigChild came back. For the very first time in as long as he could remember, he had felt some pity run down his system. He then told Ijeuwa to follow him. "What's this girl going through?" he wondered.

....

The Freeborn Slaves.

Like fourteen years ago, Ijeuwa began her story. When she was barely ten years old, her equally little cousin Echidi had come home from Port-Harcourt where she was staying with a couple as a housemaid. She looked well-fed in the eyes of the villagers who could not afford one good meal a day and she equally made mouths about it. Her cousins believed all the stories she dished to them but they never knew the agonies concealed behind the Echidi's façade and good appearances. Many of the children especially Echidi's siblings envied her and inwardly wished they could speak like her or even have the good food they thought she enjoyed.

"I won't waste time before following her to the city if she asks me," Amobi said to Ijeuwa as they were going to the stream. "See how good Echidi looks," they both agreed. They were both fantasizing and relishing what good life obtains in the cities. Their little young minds were simply on a wishful mental sojourn into the admirable city life they believed existed in the land of the stars where Echidi resided.

"At least one can eat rice and beans as one likes and…" said Ijeuwa halfway.

"And not this Fufu and Ogbono soup that we eat every day here" Amobi added cutting into her speech.

"But my mummy said" continued Ijeuwa, "that it is better to eat ashes in a house of freedom than meat in a house of slavery."

The Freeborn Slaves.

"What does that mean?" Amobi questioned.

"Mmmm, I don't know," answered Ijeuwa, "but they say that what the elders see seated, the young cannot see even standing on the highest hills. Besides, our *ogbono* and *fufu* are very delicious."

"No!" Amobi put in, "It's not just the food, Ijeuwa, this caste system in our village is just silly. Who told them that one man is superior to the other? It's just a useless and senseless culture! I hate this division that is killing everything here!" Amobi shouted throwing his hands up in total frustration.

"You really talk like you are a grown-up, Amobi," Ijeuwa said, "it's really senseless"

"Yes! They have realized the benefits of education now, and want it only for their own." Amobi put in,

"Yes, education should be the right of all, but hey... where did you learn this wisdom? Did your father teach you?" Ijeuwa praised him.

"No!" Amobi replied amidst a mouthful of mischievous laughter, "Just that when adults refuse to think right, we little kids will think right on their behalf. And teach them what right-thinking is all about." They both laughed their heads off at this.

"You are correct, my dear" Ijeuwa agreed.

The Freeborn Slaves.

"Each time I hear people say that education is the light, I cry and wonder why we can't get it. Why do we keep segregating? How can we conquer other territories or overpower invaders when we are already divided among ourselves?" Amobi queried. "One day, this invasion of our own end of the village will get to them too."

"Yes, how could they leave us to the mercy of other villagers when we all should be protected? It's just because they believe that the Owere is worth everything while Ogbodu worth nothing." Ijeuwa lamented.

"But that is just as senseless as those who believe it," Amobi fumed. "We are mixed descendants of the same man whether they like it or not. Their seeds are all everywhere in Ogbodu since they use our girls for cooling off and *mtchew*" he hissed and swallowed his speech.

"I will go and ask my father why he gave birth to me at Ogbodu!" Ijeuwa fumed.

"Yes! Amobi agreed, "We will ask them! Why are we not born at Owere? How can the Owere still be taking us for whatever they liked; men for their farms and women for their beds? They make little girl's mothers and go unpunished," Amobi went on. "Imagine! The Ogbodu little girls are good for their beds but not good enough to bear their sons."

"Hahaha," Ijeuwa laughed, "Good for bed, bad to wed. But what if our fathers cannot answer it, *mtchew*"

The Freeborn Slaves.

Ijeuwa wondered, "It is just so pathetic, maybe it's our destiny."

"I'm not with you in this one." Amobi threw in. "Is it not your father who usually said that you must stand up and fight for your rights?" Amobi reminded her.

"Yes, he says that but do we have rights here when those who think themselves privileged for noble births have hijacked our rights? They splash them freely on their own and stock them for sale to some of the same owners of the rights. That's why I ask, where has my father's fight for our rights led him?" Ijeuwa wondered. "Only troubles- not just for him but for the entire Ogbodu"

"It is not an easy task, otherwise, all the wars and fights by our people would have done that, but all we can do is fight." Amobi tried to encourage her. "If one still breathes, the best legacy is a good fight for the restoration of our dignity. Even right now, I have plans on how to liberate our people and..." Amobi continued to lecture.

"You?" Ijeuwa scoffed, "Have a plan?"

"Yes, you will see it" Amobi assured her.

"See what?" Ijeuwa queried, "Without education, you can't do a thing."

"Then let's get the education." Amobi proposed.

The Freeborn Slaves.

"Then we must leave this village," Ijeuwa suggested, "otherwise before you even grow up, we would all have died"

"No, yes, I disagree," Amobi said confusingly. "That would be like running away from one's shadows and you rightly know how possible that is."

"No, Ijeuwa disagreed. "It is better to go look for a better destiny outside than die with a bad one inside this god-forsaken village"

"I hear that the oppression of the poor in the city is even worse." chipped in a woman fetching firewood on a nearby farm. She had been so thrilled and engrossed with the wisdom from the young lips.

"Don't mind her o!" Amobi mischievously whispered into her friend's left ear. "Maybe she is one of the *Osuimi*- Monitors hahahahaaaa"

"Ah ah," Ijeuwa wondered, "but she was supporting you who said going to the city was like running away from one's shadows.''

"No, I was only joking, even I want to go to the city and you know it. I want to go to the city hahahaaa." Amobi revealed even to the confusion of Ijeuwa who was lost as to where Amobi really stood on the matter.

"For me, I'm going o I'm going to the city… Leave this enslaved land and get that education." Ijeuwa concluded.

The Freeborn Slaves.

Ijeuwa found herself in the city of Port-Harcourt full of hopes, but all that glitters are not gold. The glitters in Echidi only helped to becloud the jitters that characterize her city abode. Ijeuwa was running away from the demons but sadly into the wicked embrace of no one else but the Leviathan.

Chapter 2

"Wake up, *Akpuka-* short girl!" a harsh voice woke Ijeuwa on the first morning in the city. "Wake up before I pour this water on you!" It was the voice of her madam, a woman called De Monique standing beside her, clutching a bowl of hot water. Ijeuwa could feel the heat from the bowl as it wafted across to her.

"Good morning, ma," Ijeuwa greeted.

"What's good about this morning… eh?" Madam De Monique snapped, "What's good… when you are still sleeping by this time of the day?"

Before Ijeuwa could wipe her face properly to come to terms with the reality, "Wap!" sounded on her face and some angry fists grabbed and yanked her to her feet. "I am talking and all you could do is sit there on the mat and rub your eyes?" the harsh voice continued.

Even in her little mind, she was very able to perceive that there was fire on the mountains for her in the misadventure she had begun. As she tried to wake up properly and wipe out the blinding copious stars that the slap had ignited in her waking mind, she imagined that it was probably 8 O'clock in the morning. Nevertheless, darkness still hovered everywhere as she peeped through the window blinds.

The Freeborn Slaves.

"Why are you peeping?" De Monique shouted at her. "Your mates have already fetched their madams three drums of water each and you are still here enjoying sleep"

"Ma, but it is still dark and…" Ijeuwa was saying,

"You are talking back at me, eh?" Madam De Monique shouted and gave her another dirty slap. Ijeuwa could have entered the ground out of fear.

"No, I was just…" Ijeuwa was saying,

"Sharap!" Madam De Monique shouted her down to shut up just as she dragged her up and towards the kitchen. Now go downstairs" she went on, "and walk down the street, turn left and then left again before you turn right, and then turn right and go left. There is a tap at the end of the street, to fetch water and fill these drums. Make sure you go quickly because there are clothes here to be washed! Do you hear me?"

Ijeuwa turned to see if there was another person with them being addressed but alas, it was just the two of them except for the lazy lover of her madam who was still dozing and snoring somewhere in the rooms. The children were still sound asleep in their own room too. How was she to begin, she didn't know. She was only a few hours old in the house and knew nowhere in the area and now this- it was unbelievable. In her own family, her own clothes were still being washed for her by her older siblings and here she is being commanded to go fetch water and come back to wash

The Freeborn Slaves.

clothes. She couldn't understand or believe it. She had become terrified and really shaken yet fear couldn't let her cry even though she wanted to. She confusedly stood and held both her mouth and ears to stop the impending explosion of rain of tears and the resounding resonance of a deafening slap.

As she stood wondering what it all meant, De Monique grabbed her ear to drum the seriousness of the errand she was given and that was how the story started from the age of about fourteen through her eighteenth birthday and till this very day at Booty-for-all Paradise.

There were days she was starved for the flimsiest excuses like water spilling on the table while she brought food for Madam De Monique and her children or for not telling her that a particular food item had finished. She was the relief for Madam De Monique after each squabble with her live-in lover-husband. She owns the apartment thus the lazy man doesn't have the authority to question her.

On a particular day, before she turned eighteen, her madam bit her until she fainted. It took the miraculous intervention of a neighbor who happened to come in just then as De Monique was about to hit her with the wooden pestle to save her life. The neighbor fought her and carried Ijeuwa off on his shoulders. "Your name says it all!" the neighbor had fumed as they exchanged verbal. "You are demonic indeed!

....

The Freeborn Slaves.

"This can't be true!" Ijeuwa thought when she recovered later on in her rescuer's home. "I must be in a nightmare! But this nightmare has lasted too long and must be stopped. I must wake up from it! What's all this?!" she wondered aloud.

Worse still, the Echidi whom she had followed to this hellish place they fantasized as the city of the stars, was equally nowhere to be found. She never saw her again or even their big sister Chezo who brought both of them to Port Hacourt, soon after they arrived Port-Harcourt. Echidi was promptly forced away by a fat woman who made her shrink as soon as she saw her. Now she could imagine why Echidi shrunk like that then. "My greatest ordeal is that I have no one to complain to." Ijeuwa sobbed.

Late in the night of the third day, Ijeuwa ran away taking nothing with her and leaving no trace of her whereabouts. One thing led to the other and she found herself in Lagos and now in the arms of naughty men of Booty-for-all Paradise who derive pleasure in things even more despicable and naughtier than they themselves. According to the Booty-for-all girls, those were the ignoble officers in noble offices who stole public funds and squashed them on frivolities and ignominious sprees leaving the rightful owners of the wealth in agonizing penury.

Though they give them the money, this attitude always infuriated and disgusted the little girls of the Booty-for-all paradise. For the men, it's part of the play after hard work.

The Freeborn Slaves.

Chapter 3

"This caste story again?" BigChild fumed incredulously. "You mean you are an Osu?" He asked Ijeuwa.

"Yes, now... I mean yes, sir. Do you know what it means?" she asked but BigChild didn't bother to answer her.

"Come to think of it," BigChild reflected, "these ones have senses... and conscience too, yet they are looked down upon and talked down. Many people are really silly and need some harsh lessons! This world is a small place indeed. I never knew I had my own kind here all the while. Now my steps must hasten like I never envisaged," he agreed in himself.

Meanwhile, the man Okpeke is a card-carrying member of the Booty-for-all paradise and must be fully satisfied. The problem was that Okpeke was insisting that Ijeuwa who started the work in him must finish it. But then, as they say, mercy overrides justice thus BigChild whose spark of mercy had been ignited, got furious with Okpeke. And defying all the protocols and rules of the Booty-for-all Paradise, ordered Okpeke out of the "paradise". "He might equally be one of those caste advocates," he concluded.

"Someone must deal with all these people." BigChild continued to fume. "I've been bad right, but surely better than some people; after all I'm equally a byproduct of this. This has gone on for too long and I have the time on my hand

The Freeborn Slaves.

now. I either choose to wake up with the defeated or break up and be elevated"

Before this time, BigChild had only come to the La Medina- the Booty-for-all Paradise to attend to the applications tendered by those who had applied for a vacancy he said existed there. He had those who could handle the job but he needed fresh people now. He was sitting leisurely just across the bush bar overlooking those at the poolside, perusing one of the resumes when Everestus came to disrupt his attention.

Now he had barely recovered from this when KE came in with a rude arrogance in his breath and face. He had read about the vacancy yesterday in the Minute Post- the evening newspaper. The advert said;

>"Have you got what it takes?
>
>Don't be Lilly-livered!
>
>Hefty men and women
>
>Swift Gunners

The G was superimposed on R so you are right to read it as Gunners or Runners.

>We have a place for you!"

The qualities needed followed.

When KE read the advert, he considered all the attributes needed for the job and chose the G instead of the R. "Runners

The Freeborn Slaves.

can go to hell, he fumed. "But come to think of it, he quickly remembered, "Gunners are Runners and vice versa. It is either they are running their guns or "gunning" their runs; anyways, they are doing the same thing."

Don't Run Gun! was the inscription on the polo shirt that KE chose this morning as he prepared to go for the interview. The T-shirt had become his favorite after he craftily changed the inscription to "Don't Run. Gun!"

When BigChild saw KE enter, he supposed that the fellow must have missed his way. "He can't be our customer of course, and hmmn, he better not be an applicant or he will get the beating of his life this time," he concluded. "Besides, whoever allowed him in in the first place is already jobless."

"Hi" KE greeted, but BigChild only adjusted his glasses and kept looking into the paper in his hands, though attracted by the hoarse voice he couldn't have believed came from the tiny man if another had told him. Looking at KE, even you would have thought like BigChild too, but the truth is, KE didn't miss his way. In fact, he had been missing his abode and had just actually come where he belonged.

What's this big-headed mosquito doing here? Bigchild had thought. KE had such a disproportionate size, enormous drum-sized head on a tiny chest that arouses your pity for him and his tiny legs if you should think of an emergency arising just then, and then imagine the heavy load of his head on his tiny legs. How would he manage to run with it?

Tony Ik Odoh

The Freeborn Slaves.

Nothing was in the right place on KE's body except his heartless heart and his blaring voice.

After saying "Hi" the second time and still no response from BigChild, it was time KE lost his cool and taught "this big for-nothing cheat as KE had put it, "a lesson or two." With the speed of lightning, KE dispossessed BigChild of the papers as well as the glasses while hollering at the same time. "What the hell do you think you are, huh? I've been standing here talking and all you do is keep looking at this damn thing through these damn things," he blared demonstrating with his hands as he said "through these damn things which had referred to the papers and BigChild's sunglasses.

Everywhere had become calm- instantly calm. Nobody there could have believed that the hoarse thunderous voice was that of the tiny thing before them if they were not witnesses. Even BigChild could not believe it happened to him.

"Answer me, now!" KE blared on. "Who wants swift gunners? Do your eyes deceive you or do you underrate me?"

At this point, someone who had come in also to enquire about the vacancy heard him ask for gunners and touched his shoulders to correct him that it was runners and not gunners. He had thought it was a typographic error just like many others who never knew it was a hoax meant to catch only the right guy. Immediately the enormous hands touched KE to correct him, KE turned and ignoring the size of the man-mountain standing behind him, landed him a deflating punch

The Freeborn Slaves.

that sent the man sprawling on the ground and writhing in pain. "Gunners! Not runners, okay?" KE said as he spat on the man. The man just looked on from the ground as KE howled and growled at the same time at him; "Size is not everything!"

BigChild was enthralled and confused at the same time by all that KE had displayed in just a moment and only looked on. Inwardly, he admired the tiny man who was dramatizing before him.

"How could this ugly-looking little brat be doing all these magics with such an incredible lightning speed?" he wondered. "Where is the strength coming from? Maybe this brat remains at home o!" He laughed in real admiration. "Even to knock down this fat cow that came looking for runners? Does this place look like a stadium to him? *Mtchew*, idiot!" he hissed. BigChild had found his treasure in the tiny brat standing before him, and the search project closed.

As all this was going on, the security had come around to take orders from BigChild but he only signaled to them and they left. Ahuekwe, the man who was knocked down was left more confused when the security left without arresting "this manner-less bull" as he had put it. He made to ask why but, "Ssssss", came from BigChild, "We don't condone noise here!" He warned. As Ahuekwe wanted to remind BigChild that an animal just fought him, BigChild ordered the security to arrest him for breaking the rule of decorum.

The Freeborn Slaves.

....

Now, on his way to The Legends Bar, another of his father's outfits in the Islands, BigChild spotted Ezenobi standing with a man just a few meters away from the new Victory Islands roads. Ezenobi is the cause of his present condition of aloneness. He and his wicked royal generations were the only cause of the many sleepless nights and trauma he had suffered throughout his days and all through his village's history. He was sure it was the same face in almost the same attire he had seen that fateful black night. BigChild had adjusted his spectacles to convince himself he was not hallucinating and there he was- Ezenobi.

A wise son kills what killed his father before what killed his father kills him, he reasoned. But is it actually revenge? No! he agreed. It is a fixing of the menace at home by fixing those who destroyed the home front. A man should not be at home and allow his goat to deliver still tethered, he agreed. "Today is a special day, he said, and even the air tells me it's time."

As he sat alone thinking about all that had happened that day, his mind drifted back to events of the past and all that his father told him- the misery of his people at Ogbodu village, the destruction, and gruesome murder of all his grandfather's family in one black night. And an attempt to wipe out his own very family. The memory alone was enough to ignite the spark of his indebtedness to his family. Yes, he believed he must revenge. Why a total wipeout always he wondered. This time, they won't know what hit them.

The Freeborn Slaves.

Chapter 4

It was the usual Orie market day. People had all gone to the market except for the *Igwe*- the king, his palace guards, and some of his cabinet members. They usually stayed behind to guard the village against any invader. Right from its inception, the Orie market had remained the envy of the numerous villages that surrounded Owere village. It stood out as the gold of all markets around. Myths had it that the people who instituted the market had called some dwarfs, who performed many rituals, chanted many incantations, and poured libations on top of a fatted he-goat. Afterward, their chief priest carried the sacrificial goat around the area that was marked out for the market. They believed the saying that it is by round-trip-marketing that hegoat is sold, thus they carried the sacrificial hegoat around the area marked out for the market. By so doing, they said they had spiritually sold the market to the land of the spirits, and thus no mortal could destroy it. Since then, every attempt by the villages around to destabilize or crumble the Orie market had always met rock-defeat.

Now, the market has grown and the space has become so small for the population. The people had to leave as early as the first cockcrow to secure a place to display their items and produce.

It was on such a day and most people had left early to do their business leaving behind the king- *Igwe* Agbara and some of his cabinet men. He was just a ready-to-explore

The Freeborn Slaves.

exuberant young man who had inherited the throne from his late father.

That morning, he was sitting in his palace with his hangers-on enjoying a keg of some fresh palm wine and yet waiting for Okoro, one of the palm wine tappers, to bring his own daily ration for the day. It was customary for the selected palm wine tappers, Okoro, Orji, and Nkpa, to bring one and a half kegs of palm wine each for the king and the palace. It was not for free though, since they were paid some paltry sum, and were also compensated for the rest with the many palm trees they tapped as well as the royal favors they received whenever they had disputes with another villager. People feared going into any form of dispute with them because they always won their cases. Besides, since food poisoning was always rampant, it was a highly revered honor that one could be entrusted with the king's life.

Not quite long after Okoro, the last to bring his ration for the day left, the king spotted a pretty maiden passing by. Like his ilk, he was known for his randy behaviors and so it was no surprise when he summarily asked for the little girl to be brought to him. His aides immediately brought Omanebu, the little girl, to him. Few of the cabinet men frowned at this behavior of his, but there was nothing anyone could do. Igwe Agbara the king never sought nor took any advice from anybody in that regard especially when it concerns "my property" as he referred to the slaves- the "*Osu*". Besides, many of the cabinet men were birds of a feather and

The Freeborn Slaves.

sycophants who sang his praises even when he committed the worst of crimes just because of what they hoped to gain.

A few weeks later, Omanebu came crying. She stood at the entrance to the palace. Her appearance depicted that of the most dejected rejected creature in the whole world. She knew what she had been put into, and her mother had also explained it to her. But they still had to tell the king about it no matter what. As an Osu, she could not go into the palace unless invited by the king and that was even a privilege that only her gender and age won her. She deliberately chose to come on an Orie day when many people must have gone to the market. She had a tall hope to be invited in by the king- Igwe Agbara considering her background. As luck would have it, her expectation was not long in waiting but it was for a different reason. One of the king's aides came to enquire why she had to stand there when she was uninvited. She told him that she wanted to see the king. It surprised the boy how and why Omanebu- an Osu could summon such courage.

"To come uninvited?" The guard shrugged his shoulders, as he couldn't believe his eyes and ears. The male Osu is not welcomed at all to the palace but their female may be welcomed depending on how young and succulent they look. Still, ordinarily, the guard would have been happy to take Omanebu to the king knowing who he was with women. But the mood he saw Omanebu told him that all was not well- in fact, it frightened him. Before they could figure out whether to tell the king or not, Igwe Agbara had sent another

The Freeborn Slaves.

aide to go fetch the two of them from the entrance. The aides advised Omanebu to wipe her face clean and cheer up if she hoped to attract the king's attention.

As soon as they entered, Igwe Agbara gulped down the last drop of his palm wine and went in with Omanebu. When they had done it, Igwe Agbara realized for the first time that the little girl had been crying.

"This is not the first time now, why are you crying?" he asked wondering what her pains were.

"My mother said I'm pregnant for you" she had said.

"Eh, what do you mean?" the king flared up. "What did you just say? Do you know the sacrilege you have just spoken with your mouth?" He continued. "Don't let people hear that! It seems you don't know who you are. But I will do you the kindest favor to remind you. You are an Osu! If you don't know what it means, go ask your useless mother or father. You are our property and we choose to do with you whatever we deem fit."

"Hey, I'm finished" she cried.

"You can't bear my child now, aaah, ***Ezechitoke aju-***--may the gods forbid! The king bragged. "Anyway, because I'm in a good mood today, I am only going to warn you for the last time, never come anywhere near this palace again. Are you the first Ogbodu girl to become pregnant? See me o. better go and do whatever you like with that cursed thing

The Freeborn Slaves.

you are carrying in there. And I am sure your parents know the consequences if I should hear any of you talk about this matter again."

"My child is not cursed," Omanebu said under her breath as she cried.

"Don't be obstinate o!" the king hollered. "and don't incur my wrath! In fact, guards! Come and bundle this nuisance out!" He ranted while Omanebu continued to cry even as the aides came to drag her out of the palace. The palace chiefs who were around were confused. They couldn't understand how sweet honey turned sour. Nevertheless, they still made fun out of it. As Igwe Agbara rambled on, Omanebu kept crying and maintaining that her unborn child was not cursed even as she went home.

Some weeks later, the village was rife again with the news that Igwe Agbara had impregnated yet another girl in the village. This time, it was a daughter of the soil as they called those from the Owere side of the village. The girl Okwuoma and her parents were overjoyed because they had become related to the royal family. Quickly, marriage rites were performed and she became one of the king's queens.

In due time, the kid-women gave birth to their sons; Omanebu to Ifedili and Okwuoma to Onyeze. Onyeze later took over the mantle of leadership after the king Igwe Agbara died. He became another Igwe Agbara with the Igwe Ogbuzulu of Owere as his special title.

The Freeborn Slaves.

Chapter 5

The sole reason why Ifedili was sent to school was for him to be done away with. Those days in Owere village, it served as punishment and a sign of contempt for the slaves to be sent to school; that they would be punished by the white men and thus be done away with. They were part of the village property and could be treated with any measure of cruelty. Sometimes it was even worse than that meted to domestic animals. They were used as objects of play and entertainment for the royal family and their guests and friends. Though unknown to Ifedili how lucky he was, they all believed he went to school to be done away with in the process of learning "this inexplicable language" from these white elements from god-knows-where who speak through their nose. On the other hand, their sons and daughters whom they cherished were kept at home, away from the white man's canes.

"Who could understand what these white elements speaking through their noses are saying if not the Osu who are no better elements?" they usually asked,

At a tender age, Ifedili was sent to school. This was because he looked just like his father the king Igwe Agbara. When the time came for the next school enrollment, the king, when asked to name the people who would be enrolled, only had the joy of naming Ifedili as one of them. Every protest that he was still very tender rammed into concrete walls, as the king was adamant in his resolve to send Ifedili to school. He

The Freeborn Slaves.

made it clear to his cohorts that he was not going to kill his own blood' "this wicked reminder of some some some escapades", he always stammered, but the white man's cane would. Cane was the only thing they saw from the schools then.

Ifedili went to school and excelled. He won the hearts of many teachers in the school and particularly the heart of Rev. Mr. Green, their Religious Studies teacher who had christened him Erics. The man Mr. Green took him to London when he retired and was repatriated.

Erics graduated in medicine from a London university. He worked in Manchester for many years before deciding to come home and settle. He had indeed made money and needed to come and develop his own home. The Whites of London often made jest of him and other black people and cajoled them to go home and develop their own place. The white people usually wondered why and how even those who were privileged should transport their wealth to some already developed places rather than use it to develop their own lands. "These black men are really daft", they usually said.

Meanwhile, over there, slavery and the slave trade had been abolished. Nobody owned anybody anymore and since the proclamation was universal, Erics thought that he was already a free man in his Ogbodu village. "I really have to go and live the joy of freeborn", he had thought as he put his right leg into the taxi that drove him to the airport with his

The Freeborn Slaves.

luggage. Yes, he had to go and rejoice with his people and live a free man. And two, he was equally running away from some desperate women.

The Freeborn Slaves.

The Freeborn Slaves.

Chapter 6

After long years of sojourn in a foreign country, Erics came back home. Rude shock is a bad thing but choking bewilderment is even worse. Erics was choked by the rude surprise of what he saw and this shocked him to the marrow. His biological father, the king Igwe Agbara had died but the new king was still unleashing terror on the Ogbodu people. Nothing had changed and he felt grossly disappointed. There are more than two worlds and I never knew, he asserted as he reminisced on the different worlds he had seen overseas and the one in his village.

People still treated him with scorn and resentment. There was nothing like enthusiasm from his villagers for his return as he and the white friends had all expected. He had expected that his village would have become aware that the slave trade was over and that people would have become wiser and more modern in their thinking and way of life. But what greeted him was suppression and oppression, abject poverty everywhere, and worse still, cold reception from even his own Ogbodu people- the few that dared to come near him. Others even said in his hearing that they thought he was dead. There was frustration and backwardness in everything he could behold and he couldn't comprehend it.

The timidity resulting from ignorance and oppression by the Owere people had really dealt them a deflating blow and enslaved their mentality. They insinuated that since Erics was still alive and had lived all those years with the white

The Freeborn Slaves.

people, he must have become like them. They claimed that some of the white men had dropped their Bibles, and engaged in adulterous acts with the little girls, people's wives, and forceful snatching of valuables. The white men saw all the atrocities going on in the village but turned a blind eye to them since the king and his palace chiefs allowed them to freehand with the village palm oil, coal, and timber. What's good for the goose is also good for the gander, was how Mr. Dopehead the white man who slept with one of the Igwe Ogbuzulu's queens replied when he was confronted him.

Every hope Erics had that his people would come and welcome their illustrious son as he thought he was, who had become a medical doctor and had seen it all was lost. Even his mates who went to school with him then were not helping matters as they all stopped school when the white men and their schools were sacked from the village. Everywhere still looked cold and old with the coldness of a deserted godforsaken graveyard. To his greatest dismay, just then, one of the *Osuimi* Monitors placed by the Igwe passed by. A man mentally enslaved is afraid. He cannot think clearly. He cannot learn. He cannot develop. And that's what had happened to my people, Erics cried.

However, in all these, Erics still had his plan right in his head. He has to bring the needed development to his two-in-one village of Owere and Ogbodu. He had the plan of a state-of-the-art general hospital, and a water borehole. He believed he had a call to make his people have a true taste of

The Freeborn Slaves.

the meaning of a good life. Many people from his clan advised him against his plan. They warned him that Owere was still the same village he used to know back in the day. He refused to be daunted insisting that by the time he was through with the project, all the villagers especially the Owere villagers would be made to think twice. They would know that something good can come out of Ogbodu, as he usually puts it.

Amacha, his friend particularly, reminded him that the Ogbodu people didn't have large plots of land where he would carry out a project of the magnitude he had described. And that was when Dr Erics dropped the bombshell.

"I'll go to Owere and ask them for a piece of land", he firmly stated.

Amacha could not reply to this. He sincerely believed that Erics was really out of his mind to even allow such impossibility cross his mind. He simply cleaned his bum and was about to leave when Erics called him back. "Have I said anything to upset you?" he asked bewildered.

"Nooo", Amacha replied, just that I don't know what to say to what you just said, so I guess the best thing is to go feed my goats."

"Ok, listen, Dr Erics began, I have a plan."

The Freeborn Slaves.

"A plan?" Amacha wondered, "That would take you to that palace? Hmm, that's a suicidal plan for a shameful end, my dear."

"No, see what I want to do, Erics tried to clarify. "I would start treating sick people in my home here, and I am sure" he went on, "that when the people see how effective and curative my medicines are, they would all be rushing here to beg me to cure all their numerous diseases", he hoped, "and then, I would demand a place to build the hospital which I'm sure they won't refuse."

This sounded logical enough to Amacha so he gave in since his own personal experience proves the doctor's claim true. Dr. Ifedili had given him medicine for arthritis and waist pain that had plagued him for ages and the ailment left him after few doses. Trust Amacha, he had gone about the entire Ogbodu village spreading the good news of what the doctor had done for him.

The same goes for Okankwu who became unable to swallow *fufu*- a local delicacy after falling from a Ugba tree and had his neck fractured. Dr. Erics came to his aid; straightened his neck and cured him.

The other day, Dr. Erics had purposely added alum to some dirty water in Amacha's presence. That was the method he used to purify the bad water in the village. Amacha was there and had seen him put some gray substances in the water but he never gave a hoot about it. It was when Ujunwa his friend Dr. Erics's wife began to pour out the water that he shouted,

The Freeborn Slaves.

Eweee! How did you wash the water? *A na asazi mmiri asa-* Is water washable? he queried.

To them, there was no way one could wash water. Amacha was so overwhelmed with joy and like always, he went about doing good- preaching and spreading the good news about a doctor that washes and heals water. Before long, people had nicknamed Dr Erics, **Osaa mmiri**- Water washer. Erics had to teach the villagers how to purify water using alum'.

Now seeing the goodies in all that the doctor had been doing for them, the Ogbodu people all rallied around their own whom they had actually come to see as an illustrious son indeed. Dr. Erics cured so many diseases that his home had become a pilgrimage center of some sort. The people kept following him like they followed Jesus Christ for him to change two loaves of bread and five fish into dozens of baskets of bread and fish. They were not to be blamed though since as the saying goes, the goat naturally follows he who has the fodder. The people have the ailments and he has the cure.

In all these, one thing was outstanding, and Amacha was quick to point it out. Even though many people trooped into the doctor's house from Ogbodu and other villages, no single person came from the Owere side of the village- not even one. This truly shocked Dr. Erics when Amacha told him of his observation.

……………………..…………………………………..;…

Tony Ik Odoh

The Freeborn Slaves.

Yes, his medicine was working and his charge was fair and the people attested to it. He was happy that he was gradually fulfilling his life ambition. Dr. Erics usually went to the developed cities around to replace his stock of medicine and buy other necessary items. As all these wonderful happenings continued to take place at the Ogbodu end of the two-in-one community, they were not hidden from the ears of the Owere villagers. Some of them were already longing for a chance to be part of the many goodies they heard emanated from the Ogbodu clan.

"How comes the sensible suddenly becomes the senseless?" some Owere youth wondered. "We claim to be the wise real humans, how come we still left dangerous diseases to ravage our land when the solution to our problem lies just within arm's reach?" So many of the younger ones were already getting pissed by the whole thing but the youths were not given a voice in matters of their tradition, thus they simply waited for the god that sent the saving Dr. Erics to Ogbodu to send them theirs.

Chapter 7

Just before driving into the village on one of his visits to the city, Dr. Erics was stopped by Ichie Agu. Ichie Agu was a member of the king's cabinet and had deliberately stood at the Owere entrance waiting for the doctor's arrival.

Only two people owned motorcycles in the entire village- the royal family and Dr. Erics. Dr. Erics owned a motorcycle as well as a Colt car. The sound of the doctor's motorcycle as it revved in the early morning air usually woke them from their sleep. It also announced the doctor's trip to the cities. He usually had to leave early in the morning in order to be able to come back within some days.

With fear and trembling, Ichie Agu waited for his salvation. On sighting Dr. Erics, he looked left and right before finally flagging him down. Then with a heart that trembled and pounded like it would break the rib cage, he informed Dr Erics about the obvious- the king in council, the elders, and the people passed a decree and swore to an oath that whoever patronized Dr. Erics would be ostracized, and sent to exile for seven years. He also informed him that the council swore that nobody should have anything to do with him in the village but that since they were outside the Owere soil, he felt in his mind that he was no longer under the oath hence he could talk with him. After all the preambles, Agu stated his real motive for stopping him; he begged to be treated for a chronic cough that has lived with him all his life. This made Dr. Erics's face beam with a smile.

The Freeborn Slaves.

First was the information. At least, he has become sure that the Owere people were not unaware of the goings-on in the Ogbodu village.

Secondly, he was happy to realize that they were interested in his services but were only being restricted by some wicked laws of wicked leaders. He knew that their endurance would wear out after some time.

Thirdly, they had expected that their link would come whenever the youth revolt but now their link is from a palace chief instead. A member of the council is asking to be treated? It was very heartwarming. He would be a living witness to the others. Even the trainee nurse from a nearby village who was with Dr. Erics was overwhelmed with the development. She couldn't believe her eyes that a council member was practically interested in their medicine.

With joy and happiness, Erics opened his medicine box and gave Agu some medicines from the stock he had just bought. He confirmed that Ichie Agu had eaten before they moved further to a nearby spring where Agu fetched some water with which he gulped the medicine down to his stomach. After ascertaining how to take them, Agu hid the remaining under a nearby dwarfish young palm tree, for the next days' doses. He dared not take it to the village- he was under oath.

Agu was overwhelmed with the hospitality and kindness shown to him by a "despicable" Osu. As he turned to go home, he pondered and brooded over who the wise or superior one was- they or the doctor. They are the ones who

The Freeborn Slaves.

have the sicknesses but refuse to be treated with the cure the doctor is willing to offer. The diseases won't kill the doctor as he doesn't have them. "But still, I think our tradition should stand anyway. In fact, I am confused" he shrugged and looked back to be sure that the doctor didn't hear his thoughts.

Dr. Erics went home and narrated his encounter with Ichie Agu to his wife Ujunwa and his friend Amacha. They were all happy and believed that being a palace chief, Agu would convince his fellow chiefs to change their stance. "God has a way of doing things o," they rejoiced. "This is the link we've been praying for," they all enthused. "Yes, it is!" Erics affirmed, "Good thing can come from an Osu after all."

The Freeborn Slaves.

Chapter 8

The medicine worked like magic on Ichie Agu- thanks to a few visits to the stream and the growing palm tree. At the subsequent cabinet meetings, Agu would quickly retort "How can I?" against insinuations that he may have compromised on their agreement against Dr. Erics. At other times he would say, "It is *Ezechitoke* our God that healed me!" if anyone asked him how his trademarked cough got cured.

It truly should be surprising because Agu's cough had been a nuisance during cabinet meetings. They couldn't understand how and neither could they believe that for any reason, such an age-long nuisance would just agree to develop wings and fly away leaving such a safe haven as Agu's throat. It was unbelievable considering how every creature treasures its habitat. Ichie Agu's type of cough was a factory-fitted one from his personal god, especially and specifically designed to fit and reside perfectly at his throat. It was a funny nuisance the cabinet men enjoyed each time he let go of the earth-quaking sound from his throat. It was insuperable and defied all herbs. Now the thing is so gone that a fellow chief became very confrontational someday and demanded that Agu told them the herbalist and his shrine where he got cured for the benefit of other villagers plagued by such diseases. At the height of the accusations, Ichie Agu reminded them of the oath and asked them to let the god of their land fight his own battle.

The Freeborn Slaves.

Everyone was surprised including his wife because of the sudden disappearance of such a branded cough. She was happy but confused about the cure, and since her husband was not forthcoming with the origin of the cure or the story about how the miracle happened, she simply let the sleeping dog lie. After all, she had lived with her husband all these years to know him well. "He must have done it one way or the other," she thought. "And the Doctor's medicine is in fact, the only viable option" she concluded.

The Freeborn Slaves.

Chapter 9

Dr. Erics and friends waited for quite some time for Agu's healing to bring the expected dividend, but it was not forthcoming. After waiting some time more, then it was time for him to make his move. He had to visit the palace. He agreed with his wife to visit "and state my case before them all" he had said as he stamped his feet on the floor. He nearly bypassed his friend Amacha saying that he- Amacha would simply go down the memory lane to remind him of all the things he had termed unimportant and only good for the garbage bin.

When he was about to leave, he convinced himself that he would just tell Amacha about his mission just to fulfill all righteousness- "After all he is my friend and probably the only friend at that" he thought. He assured himself that no matter what reason Amacha might tender, it would be unable to dissuade him from going to see the king and his council.

Amacha did not betray his friend's trust and expectations anyway- not at all. On hearing of a proposed visit to the palace this second time, Amacha was shocked beyond words. He had ruminated over it after the first time and found Agu's inability to show up with the needed link as an indicator that it wasn't feasible and he expected that his friend could have caught the gist as well. He found this second time thought by Dr. Erics unbelievable to have come from his well-read friend. When he came to, all he did was sing **"Al'Owere anyi o"** the usual derogatory song with

The Freeborn Slaves.

which the Owere people taunted them. That was a song that told stories of the greatness of the Owere people and their resources. A song that enthroned the humanness of the Owere people and the inhumanness of the Ogbodu people. It also stressed the need to weaken Ogbodu and subjugate their lineage. That was part of the crafty machinations of the selfish Owere people; a derogatory song of contempt with which the Owere people castigated the Ogbodu people as inferior and useless stock of people who were neither sons nor daughters and thus should be killed and thrown away.

The song was usually sung during festivals such as **Okike**- in respect of their creator, **Akatakpa** and **Echaricha**- the harvest time masquerades festivals, moon, and yam festivals, etc. During such festivals, the true sons and daughters of the village gather at the village square, to dance, rejoice, and make merry. Those days, it was usually full of fun as they all gathered to watch their young men wrestle while the young maidens sang to cheer their heroes and prayed to their gods and goddesses for victories for their admired heroes and those they secretly prayed and wished to be their husbands. It also used to be the time they entertained their special guests with the "an eye for an eye" contest. Young agile youths from the Ogbodu village were chosen and given dangerous weapons to fight themselves and only one was allowed to come out of the arena alive. The festivals were usually marked with full-geared fun-fare as they relished the days' activities and also watched their numerous masquerades perform.

The Freeborn Slaves.

There was equally the day at the "Arena of No Challenge", where the village comedians sat under the ***Udala*** and ***Uvuru*** trees to thrill their audience. They were allowed to tell any type of hyperbolic lies with no one allowed to challenge or question the truthfulness. The highest one was allowed to do was to simply exclaim *"huuuuuu, huuuuuu"* in a bid to show your doubt about a particular claim.

Two notable comedians existed in their history who have refused to be forgotten- Onam and Ochefube. Onam was a visually impaired one-legged old man who claimed he went hunting and was confronted by a pride of seven lions. According to him, he was already done with a disappointing hunting experience and was miserably on his way home. He had wasted all his arrows and gunpowder thus he had only two arrows left for his bow. Now, seeing the carnivores, he didn't know what to do but still he knew he must do something. Thus he claimed he had put the two arrows in the one bow and fired at once. As he fired, he claimed he had equally rolled himself across the ground over to the place where the lions were, thus killing all two by his arrows and the remaining five as he rolled over them. *"Huuuuuu, huuuuu"* was all the people shouted as they all wondered how a one-legged visually impaired old man could have gone hunting in the first place, let alone achieve such a feat. They laughed until tears poured from their eyes.

On the other hand, Ochefube had claimed that he would support Wembaforce at Adishi-Agwa in what was later translated to mean Wilberforce's "World Conference" when

The Freeborn Slaves.

he would raise the issue of abolishing the slave trade. He claimed that the singular support would keep slavery away from their land thus bringing sanity and peace to Owere land. The people all wondered with mouths agape as they wondered who or what Wembaforce and Adishi-Agwa meant. None had ever heard such names before and they equally knew that Ochefube was a comic lunatic who had never left the shores of their village. He claimed he had the **Amusu-** witch spirit, which gives him extrasensory perception powers. He said he could call names of people who existed in generations to come and even in other lands that were yet unknown to his villagers. The sounds of those names and other such names he called usually made them shiver and wonder how and where he manufactured them. It was he who had called the name Maraya Selenso way back before Mary Slessor was even born. The Villagers only got to connect the two names later on in history when they heard Mary Slessor and compared it with the mythological name, Maraya Selenso, and "Sukot" to probably be Ochefube's version of Scotland.

Indeed, the celebration had various activities and food delicacies prepared for each day's occasions and those were only meant for the pleasure of the treasured Owere indigenes.

On the other hand, the Ogbodu people being Osu, of a lower stock and the property of the Owere people were not allowed to partake in the fun-filled festivals and merry-making. They were not even allowed to watch them enjoy themselves let

The Freeborn Slaves.

alone be a part of it. It was seen as the greatest taboo for an Osu to even set eyes on the Owere people or their masquerades performing during the festivals. The Owere people claimed that the eyes of the Osu were defiled and thus should not be allowed to behold anything hallowed or sacred. That was because according to the Owere folktales, many of the Osu, their slave ancestors, and their generations yet unborn were sacrifices already offered to the village idols and deities.

But the aroma of food afar off makes the mouth salivate just like the melodies of instruments and sonorous voices afar off make the upper eyelid tremble in the joy of expectance. In the same way, those of the Ogbodu people who could not starve their ears and eyes of such favored flavors of leisure pleasure, joy, and merriment hid behind their palm-frond-fences and peep, hence the song *"Al Owere anyi o"* asking why is the Osu watching them through their palm frond fences.

Meanwhile, as they watched from behind their fences, they as well made sure nobody from the Owere saw them. As they peeped, they bore in their minds what consequences awaited them, should they be seen or caught stealing sight. They knew that to be caught peeping meant severe punishment or even death for the defaulter and the confiscation and destruction of the little properties he or she owned.

The Owere people drummed it into the ears of their offspring, the claim that the eyes of the Osu were defiled

The Freeborn Slaves.

because they were sacrifices dedicated or already sacrificed to idols. They said that the Osu eyes would desecrate their masquerades and festivals, thereby offending their gods and goddesses if they were allowed to be part of the celebration in any form. They were not even allowed to pound anything in their mortars so as not to attract attention to themselves.

Even in the streams, someone from Ogbodu was not to fetch water when an Owere indigene was a few meters away even unknowingly. They usually had to shout well ahead of time to announce their arrival at the streams so as to ensure they didn't fetch water alongside the Owere son or daughter.

There was the case of a man whose son had some kind of fever during a masquerade festival. The sound of the pestle and mortar, as he pounded herbs, was heard by some of the village monitors who went straight to the palace and reported it to the king. They even twisted the story, and claimed they saw the man pounding yam.

The king summarily ordered the arrest of the accused and the immediate burning of his household and property. He warned them that there should be no excuse whatsoever not to carry out his order to the letter.

"What insolence?! Why should he dare me?" he fumed. "He wants to desecrate the gods of our land or what? *Mba nu!* No! A child should not lift up his father else the incredible things from the father's yonder would blind him." He fumed, "Bring him here for me! He wants to implicate me and my elders, but I will teach him a bitter lesson today!

The Freeborn Slaves.

He continued ranting and panting even as the guards and errand boys had left.

When a wicked man is on the throne, the people suffer. The guards went, saw but couldn't conquer. They couldn't conquer themselves. They couldn't conquer the falsehood in their minds neither could they conquer the glaring truth that was staring them in their faces. They couldn't conquer their faceless tradition.

They saw the man pounding herbs and not yam as the false reporters had alleged. Some felt pity for him and wanted to go back and tell the king what they actually saw but remembering the threat that there should not be any excuse whatsoever, they had to carry out the king's order. They dragged the family members inside their hut and set them ablaze. Finally, they bound the culprit and took him to Igwe Agbara the king as he had demanded.

At the palace, the man Eleje was asked why, how, and where he got the yam he was pounding but he kept quiet. They tormented him to tell them why he chose to desecrate their masquerade festival but still, he didn't try to defend himself. But if the goat is pushed to the wall, he would have no option but to fight back just like the ram who though not a good dancer would not mind dancing how best he could if the music came to his abode. Now when the maltreatment and dehumanization became unbearable, he spat on the king's face and cursed him and his generation.

The Freeborn Slaves.

"I neither had yam nor pounded any," he had begun. "If it was yam that I was pounding, let *Ezechitoke* our God strike me dead, but if it was herbs that I was pounding, then let that sickness that the herb was meant to cure, kill you, your generations to come, and all those who gave you the false information." The sycophants booed him as he stated his case. "Remember," he went on, "we have all descended from Owere and he has been warning you all about the way you treat us. If it pleases God and our ancestors and progenitors that you burnt innocent people alive, then let it be, but if not, hmm… then know it that you, your family, and cohorts would continue to die by fire, painful misery, and violence. And these evils shall never depart from your home. The day will surely come… we will be strong and free ourselves from your power… and this intoxicating power will elude you."

As he was speaking, the crowd was booing him. They had not even recovered from the shock that right before them, Eleje had the effrontery to call the name of Ezechitoke- their holy God. And now he was cursing their king. They never believed that an Osu had any part with God. They laughed and made a mockery of him. They told him that an Osu was already cursed and as such cannot curse another person.

In a rage, the king signaled his chief guard, Ishiokpukpu, and his fellow head-hunters. They took Eleje to one of the evil forests and in one fel,l swoop, Ishiokpukpu cut Eleje's head.

The Freeborn Slaves.

As Amacha reminded him of all these, Dr Erics regretted ever telling him of his plans. He knew all the stories and memories but he believed that his plans would right the wrongs.

"Yes, we are all aware of these, but this project would render them obsolete and make them things that should be buried in the past." Dr Erics had begun, "I am sorry to disappoint you Amacha, my friend, because my mind is already made up and I must visit the king and his chiefs," he said with a note of finality in his voice.

"Whoever is going to allow you into the palace?" Amacha said in a voice laden with a mischievous laughter of mockery. He wondered how his friend could summon such a big courage to dream a big dream as this. But Dr Erics told him that dreaming was free and that everyone was free to dream as big as they chose. Dr Erics said that after all, it was not them that would bring the dreams to pass. "Nature has a way of conspiring and discussing within itself to bring dreams to reality," Dr. Erics had lectured, "and woe betide you if your dream was just a cheap one, you just die like the ants leaving no memory"

"So you think you will go to the palace and even be accepted well enough to make your demand?" Amacha asked unbelievingly.

"Yes, because when you dream well, the dreams come to you by themselves" .Dr. Erics replied.

The Freeborn Slaves.

"So you dream that the king and his council will come to you then?" Amacha mocked.

"Yes, and I will build my hospital" Erics answered.

Now, on his way to the king's palace, by chance again, Dr. Erics met Ichie Agu. In his usual manner, Agu looked left and right to make sure no one was near and then signaled to the doctor to meet him at the usual place. Dr. Erics who also saw that as an opportunity to find out Agu's side of the story obliged him and drove ahead to wait for him at the village entrance. They both arrived at their destination through different routes.

As soon as they got there, Agu promptly explained to him how he had been having a running stomach for more than five days now after eating a popular delicacy. As a result of the sickness, he had visibly thinned in and it showed all over him. Preparedly, Dr Erics had some doses of medicines which he promptly handed to Agu. He had carried some medicines with him for demonstration at the palace in case the need arose. He also promised to bring the remaining doses in two days' time when they had scheduled to meet again.

"Mmmm" Doc cleared his throat to attract Agu's attention but Agu was already far at home in his mind. He was contemplating whether he was a smart man or a traitor, or worse still a destroyer, destroying himself with his secret association with the doctor. Though he pretends and puts up appearances like one not perturbed by the village's threats of

The Freeborn Slaves.

the god's wrath and the consequences of the oaths, he inwardly fears the powers of the village gods. The gods were said to be left-handed and did things left-handedly and in a very negative and extreme way.

"Em, Ichie Agu" Dr Erics called again, "I was on my way to see you all at the palace when by chance we met"

Agu winked and almost betrayed himself. "Eh?" he asked pretending not to have heard what Erics who on his own didn't notice anything had said. "How could this man allow this kind of thought to even cross his mind?" Agu queried in his mind.

"I said I wanted to come and meet you all at the palace for an important discussion," Dr Erics went on not even noticing the sign of loathing for him on Agu's face. Nevertheless, after explaining his mission, he sought Agu's advice on the best way to go about it.

Yes, Agu loathed him as did every other Owere person, but he knew the benefits inherent in the doctor's association with the Owere people. He therefore informed him that the council meeting for the day was cancelled because of some reasons and pledged his genuine interest to help him in his mission. At least he knew that his own household would partake in these wonders called Whiteman's medicines. Again, he would become very free to come and be treated at the doctor's clinic without fear of any embarrassment from anybody. "That would be great!" he thought to himself. He then pleaded with Erics to be given some time to think out

The Freeborn Slaves.

the best way to go about it and since they would be meeting in two days' time, he promised to bring feedback to him then.

That sounded very logical to Erics, and since the meeting was no longer going to hold, he agreed with him. They were talking about the wrecker bird flu that was rampaging and raging in the Owere village then of which Dr. Erics had been able to almost eradicate at the Ogbodu village but which still wrecked its havoc at the Owere side. Agu was already fantasizing about how good it would be if their mission succeeded.

Even Dr Erics was so overtaken by their discussion that he left his motorcycle and walked along with Agu. They were almost inside the village together when suddenly Agu awoke from his reverie of mental fantasy and frenzy. Just then, he looked up and saw Nwite another cabinet member rushing past them. Nwite was rushing to see his father-in-law who had reportedly fallen from a palm tree and was in serious pain.

On seeing them, Ichie Nwite raised no eyebrows. He had a more urgent call to attend to than waste his precious time talking to or thinking about "this traitor" as he had put it. As he walked and ran, he wondered aloud, "No wonder the sudden disappearance of that nuisance of a cough."

Agu made to ask him where he was going, but Nwite simply ignored him and rushed past them. Then Agu knew what grave trouble he had fallen into. The situation appeared most

The Freeborn Slaves.

hopeless to him. "I can handle him," he said to himself consciously ensuring that Dr Ifedili heard him. "Ok," Dr. Erics said and they parted ways.

The Freeborn Slaves.

The Freeborn Slaves.

Chapter 10

The evening seemed to have crept onto Agu faster than any other day. He truly fidgeted when the town crier announced an emergency joint meeting of the chiefs and the elders' council. Though the urgency in the town crier's voice told a different thing some had thought it was to compensate for the one that was canceled in the morning but Agu, the guilty one was afraid. This summons for an emergency meeting took him by storm. "Why must it be Nwite that caught us… that loudmouthed he-goat" he cried. He expected the meeting but not that soon. He had hoped to talk things over with Nwite in the evening before the emergency meeting which he surely expected. He had hoped it would come maybe from the day after.

As a crooked-minded man, Agu had planned to sell to Nwite the idea of sabotaging the council's stance on the doctor's matter and enjoying the benefits of good health for himself and his household. He had as well planned other things against Nwite if he failed to see things from his angle. Nwite has a chronic backache that has lived as long as him and Agu had hoped to use that and the trick of taking the drug outside the Owere village as his selling point- "But chai… this very sudden summons for a meeting has shattered my plans!" he cried to himself. "Still, no shaking" he assured himself, "I have the will… there must be a way."

At the meeting, Agu already knew he was the sole reason for the meeting but still feigned ignorance of it. He even went to

The Freeborn Slaves.

ask Nwite how his in-law was doing but Nwite rather changed his seat than answer him.

....

"*Igweee,* you shall live forever," they all rose and chorused as their king entered. The king took his seat and signaled them to sit.

Promptly, the king cleared his throat and in a very unusual manner welcomed everyone by their respective chieftaincy titles- palace chiefs and elders alike. He then asked Nwite to repeat what he had earlier told him and he did. Nwite repeated how he was coming from the morning wine tapping and was informed that his father-in-law had fallen from a palm tree. He even explained how his calabash fell from his hands and broke because of the shock. He then explained how he was rushing to see what he could do to save his in-law when he saw "this traitor" as he had put it pointing at Agu, "and that despicable Osu Dr... em em em **Amamafaya**"- implying he does not even know doctor Erics's name, at the village gate." He said the twosome was so engrossed in their discussion that they were even holding hands. "And I stood and watched them for some time and eh... and eh... they didn't even notice me," he clarified.

On hearing this, many who were sitting close to Agu shifted from him in total bewilderment and shock. "You are defiled!" they shouted at him but Agu simply laughed and frowned at once.

The Freeborn Slaves.

"You are such an unpardonable disgrace," he said to Nwite. "You should have asked questions eh… ask me what I was doing with the man before jumping to this stupid conclusion. Do you want to tarnish my image? See how you have made the hearts of men- these honorable chiefs and distinguished elders almost jump out of their mouths with these foorr foorr foorr funny pictures you have just painted. Men should learn to be honorable o! In fact, my king, it is high time we questioned the integrity of some of our so-called chiefs"

As he made to continue his rain of abuses on Nwite, he was called to order and urged to vindicate himself instead.

Agu then went on to tell them how he was coming from the farm and overheard some market women's discussion. The women according to him were discussing how one of the women's husbands lost his fertility after taking medicine from Dr Erics. He narrated how another of the women told how she and her husband got rashes all over their bodies after their visit to the doctor's clinic. Yet another told of how her seven months old pregnancy got aborted, no thanks to the doctor's medicines.

"*Opukaa*!" cut in Opanka as Agu made to continue in his endless list of 'yet another ones'. "How does these stories concern us, my fellow chiefs?" asked Opanka, "how do they concern us?!"

The Freeborn Slaves.

"*Juanu ya nu*, ask him" supported another, "Ask him. I still remember how his cough vanished..." he recalled mischievously.

"Em, Ichie Agu" the king began, "tell us what your interest is in this whole story because none of the women you mentioned is from our Owere village"

"Yes, tell us" chorused the people.

At this, it was like the only chance Agu had been waiting for just came crashing into his waiting embrace. A crafty mind is always ready.

"That's why I said we have to screen some of..." Agu started again.

"Opukaa!" shouted Opanka again as Ichie Agu made to start abusing Ichie Nwite again. "Defend yourself man" he urged Agu.

Agu then told them how one of those women had disclosed the doctor's intention to visit the palace. He told them that Dr. Erics would be coming to ask for a piece of land on which he was proposing to build a hospital. He also told them that the women said it was a plan by Dr. Erics to get back at the Owere people for the mistreatments they had meted out to them all through the years.

"Opukaa!" shouted Opanka, "This is the height of your lies Ichie Agu!"

The Freeborn Slaves.

At this, they all concluded that Agu must be really mad to think he could sell such a cheap lie to them.

"How could Dr. Erics or whoever he calls himself even in his wildest dream conceive such a taboo in his mind?' they queried.

"An Osu?" queried one.

"To desecrate the palace or what?" queried another.

"Maybe he has gone nuts just like this man standing here before us," said another.

"Tell us a better lie… that was an unbelievable white lie not meant even for the insane," they concluded.

"He is such a bad seller" said one, "his lies are so cheap yet no one is willing to buy"

Agu laughed and asked them to bet him to it that if his claim was verified to be true, the punishment meant for him would be transferred to Nwite. He told them how he saw Dr. Erics and thought it wise to verify the women's claim that he wanted to come and demand for a piece of land from the palace. And when he had found that it was really true, all he did was pretend to be working with him so as to help him reach his waterloo quicker. He said this and laughed wryly.

"Opukaa, you have forgotten the oath? You could have waited for him to come and meet us than making an unecessary enquiry," said Ichie Opanka, "why go to meet the

The Freeborn Slaves.

talk at the gate when it would eventually meet you here? Or have you made yourself the Ashema the village provost?"

"My king?" Agu called, "You know as well as I do that the Osu have a covenant to avenge whatever we have done to them. They have a revenge-covenant that cannot be changed and and eh..." Some got convinced that it could be true, while many others dismissed it as a cock and bull story by a man already lost and confused but bent on finding a way out of the woods.

The council chose some people to go immediately and verify Ichie Agu's claims. They would rather go and see an uncondemned male Osu than allow him into their palace else he would desecrate it. The land belongs to Owere people and they were free to move wherever they wished. The emissaries were to simply say to Dr. Erics;

"At our council meeting today, Ichie Agu brought up the idea you have about having a hospital here. We saw the sense in it and have come to know how you want to go about it."

They were to watch out for signs that may suggest the idea was his or was sold to him. If they confirm the plan or idea to be truly his, they should pretend to be working with him.

Agu was visibly happy with the genius of his clever performance and so was arrogantly boasting- "After this time, we would know who is a traitor, Ichie Agu or Ichie whatever". As he bragged and pranced, the cold sweat on his

The Freeborn Slaves.

forehead was telling a different story of a man inwardly afraid. What if they suddenly find out that he had been treated by the doctor? This question in Agu's mind really scared the living daylight out of him.

As he boasted his life away, Igwe Ogbuzulu the king reminded him of the consequences of lying under oath and of making the royal council to visit an Osu for something that was not true. "It's Outright banishment!" the king concluded.

Agu affirmed he was aware of the consequence but prayed secretly that the drugs he received in the past do not give him away.

The Freeborn Slaves.

The Freeborn Slaves.

Chapter 11.

Chima was probably the only honest man among those chosen to go see Dr. Erics. He was one of the cabinet members whose integrity still stood. He was among them because he always antagonized the king and thus the king wanted to prove to him that the doctor had ulterior motives. Chima had dismissed the whole story as a mere fabrication by Ichie Agu. He knew Dr. Erics was a good man who had a genuine interest in the people and who would not harbor or do anything that would harm them. "If the doctor actually said he needed a piece of land for a hospital," he had murmured at the palace, "then it must be for a good course and not this Agu's out-of-the-blues story."

"*Opukaa*! Mr. Explainer... have you come again?!" retorted Opanka.

"What we all hear is how the doctor had been saving people," said Chima ignoring Opanka, "how can he start killing the same people he had been saving, impossible!

"What's impossible?" shouted Opanka.

"How come every other person says good things about the doctor except these women of Ichie Agu's market women?" Chima asked Opanka.

"I wonder o, my brother," Opanka replied even to the surprise of Chima and others, "but the truth will come out today," he said. "But who says everybody talks good about

The Freeborn Slaves.

your... *A*mamafaya?" Opanka fired back at Chima. In retrospect, he had suddenly realized that he supported the doctor unknowingly. Many Owere people would rather say Dr. **Amamafaya** than call the name "Dr. Ifedili or Erics". They usually referred to him as '**Amamafaya**' meaning they do not know his name just to show contempt.

....

Dr. Erics was overjoyed to have the royal people in his little home and it was written all over him. His home was the first house in Ogbodu to have corrugated iron sheets as its roof.

"How could you be coming to see me, *Ndi-Ichie anyi*- our royal chiefs?" he joyfully asked the emissaries while dusting and offering them the seats meant for his patients, "You should have waited for me to come." He was immediately showering praises on the king and his people for deciding to change into modernity. He promptly went further to tell them how he was already on his way to see them at the palace when by chance he met Ichie Agu. They could all see the sincerity on his face as he spoke. He was about to tell them of the drug he had given to Ichie Agu when,

"Hey!" Ekerue shouted and shrugged his shoulders in utter disbelief, "You mean you were already coming to the palace?"

"Yes!" Dr. Erics replied joyfully,

The Freeborn Slaves.

"You?' Opanka shuddered, "*Opukaa*! Youuuu... at the palace?"

"Yes..." the Doc had said thinking they were together. "Ichie Agu never told me he would do it so quickly and..." he continued.

"*Opuka*!" Opanka cut in again, "Wonders shall never end" he finished under his breath.

"I told you!" put in Ekerue, "The Whites... mtchew" he hissed and swallowed his words.

"I was expecting to see him in..." Dr. Erics wanted to tell them of the scheduled meeting in two days' time but the emissaries had heard more than their ears could carry.

"Okay," Ekerue and Opanka cut in simultaneously, "See you in the meeting next Afor day then," they finished and they all turned and began to leave.

"Let me offer you some kolanuts, please" he pleaded.

"Nooo, bring it with you at the next meeting," the Ashema, replied. Erics was a bit confused at the sudden departure of the council men but promptly excused it to be their realization that he actually intended to visit them at the palace. "Yes! This is good!" he rejoiced, "Things would soon take their proper places and shapes!"

"Opukaa! Hmm... Opukaa!" Opanka continued to shout and shudder as they went home.

The Freeborn Slaves.

Dr. Erics was so happy and excited that he even failed to see the hatred in the eyes of his august visitors. He so relished the joy of being visited by the royal cabinet men of Owere village that he didn't notice the evil water of hatred boiling right in their eyes. He didn't see the passionate hatred that burned in those eyes that looked at him. You wished there was a mechanism to decipher the heart's content by just looking at the face.

....

Dr. Erics's wife Ujunwa, and Amacha his friend were not deceived by the whole thing. They felt that the whole thing happened just too quickly to be all for good. They specifically didn't believe that Ekerue would be a party to anything good for the Osu. It was when they asked him what Chima said that it dawned on him that he never said anything.

"That silence speaks volumes, my Doc" Amacha said.

"Yes, I believe you," put in Ujunwa, "It says a lot my dear."

"There's much to all this that misses your eyes" Amacha cautioned.

Dr. Erics accused them of being myopic and unable to see that the whole village was on the verge of a a rampage for positive change. "I am sure Agu have told them the truth

The Freeborn Slaves.

about his cures," he asserted, "besides, they are not unaware of the happenings here"

When they could not make him change his mind, they let him have his way. "I told you is better than I would have told you" Amacha warned as he drew on his own ear to buttress his seriousness.

"I have a clean mind," replied Dr. Erics, "and so there is nothing to warn me about."

The Freeborn Slaves.

The Freeborn Slaves.

Chapter 12.

"That **Amamafaya** thinks he can hoodwink us?" Ekerue opined on their way home.

"But too, we have played our cards well there." Supported Opanka.

"When a cunning man dies, a cunning man would bury him hahahaaa," rejoiced Ekerue. They all except Chima had been discussing the matter since leaving the Doc's home.

"Honestly, I am confused" replied Opanka.

"There's nothing to be confused about," said Ekerue, "don't be deceived by all those pretenses; he can't fool me." He went on.

"I don't know where to stand" was all Ichie Nweke could say.

"You know where to stand Nweke." Ichie Chima replied speaking for the first time. "Yes, you don't know where to stand because you know where you stand. You know where to stand but your rotten mind does not allow you to exercise your willpower. You have truth stored in your mind but your lips are only shaped for lies You call some others the slaves, yet you are the real slaves. You slavishly follow what you don't actually believe in; a brutish

The Freeborn Slaves.

tradition that does you no good. It is rather preventing you from exercising the freedom you claim to have"

"Are you any better, Mr. Preacher?" Ichie Ekerue mocked him, "We are all together in it- really deep!"

"I am not any better but as for me, I must speak my mind when we get to the palace"

As Ichie Chima spoke, they all kept quiet except for Ichie Opanka's 'Opukaa' which he habitually reeled already getting irritated by Ichie Chima's sermons. His deafening silence all along had made them very uncomfortable.

"It is clear what the doctor's intentions and desires are," Ichie Chima went on, "He has a genuine intention and there are no two ways about it."

"If you preach from today till forever," Ekerue cut in, "it doesn't change the fact that doctor whatever you call him had bitten more than he could chew and is already done for."

"I am not asking you to change, Ichie Ekerue" Chima continued, "Suit yourself with whatever plans you have! All I know is that I am only going to say what I observed and you say yours. I am already ready for the consequence of that oath" he finished sternly.

Chapter 13.

At the palace, some of the chiefs were already feeling some remorse for initially thinking badly of Ichie Agu. They totally believed that Agu was right and was only working for the good of the Owere people.

As Ekerue noticed this feeling of remorse in some of their members, he reminded them that Dr. Erics was trained by the white men and had lived all those long years with them. He surreptitiously tried to align and agree with Agu's assertion that Erics might actually be on a revenge mission.

"He must have learned those tricks from them," he opined. "They present good things to you first and later come up with their original evil plan. Once bitten…"

"Twice shy," Opanka chipped in. Chima simply cast him a knowing look and ignored him.

"Come to think of it, no one has found the god they claimed lived in the sky till today" Ekerue mocked.

"Thank the gods for our Omeje, the god of war," Ekerue said in a mouthful of mischievous laughter.

The villagers believe that it was the Omeje deity that drove the white men out of Owere village. A white man, Mr Bell, was said to have gone to the Omeje shrine to steal the Omeje idol as they have done to so many other idols. On getting there, the python that guarded the wooden idol promptly

The Freeborn Slaves.

came out of its abode and bit him. The others were said to have scampered for safety. All efforts to revive Mr Bell proved abortive as he died within hours of the bite.

Chima reminded them of the goodies the doctor had brought to the Ogbodu people and the ones he planned to bring to the village and opined that an evil-minded man could not be doing all that. "We can't reject all that. Or shall we be in the river and not bathe properly? Besides, we have all come to believe that those who read can lead," he asserted.

"That's true" murmured some members though none was bold enough to speak up.

"Why not bring back those em em em, and let them teach us too instead of going elsewhere for it" suggested another.

"Ask me o!" Ichie Agu supported them, "I equally see it that way, but since I no longer have an opinion on the matter, I'd rather keep quiet"

"Better keep remaining quiet o," Ekerue hushed him down, "You haven't explained the mystery about your cough," he finished and that quickly put Agu back to his shell.

The king's anger and hatred knew no bounds now. "Right in my palace" he was thinking, "my cabinet members are showing signs that they want to side an Osu? Hmmmm… Impossible!" he shuddered and shrugged his shoulders and

The Freeborn Slaves.

said it could never happen. "Not when I'm on the throne," he thought almost aloud. It was Dr. Erics's growing popularity as against his own plummeting royal grace that worried him madly. "How can an Osu have all the things that I, Igwe the king should have exclusively?" he wondered, "I can't allow that at all, and neither will I continue to witness this abomination! He may be whatever he likes but he is still an Osu- my property"

During subsequent meetings, most cabinet members except Chima and his group when asked to air their view on the matter would paint a picture of the good in the doctor's proposal but would end by saying that they stood wherever the king stood. He noticed this and it was to his utmost displeasure.

"This can't be happening!" the king and his group agreed, "It is unpalatably unacceptable". In the end, Igwe swallowed hard and maintained that all was well and that he too had given his support. Inside him, he was nursing a chronic hatred for Dr. Erics. He accused him of usurping his position and trying to take over his kingdom with his 'self-styled- messianism' as he had put it.

Just like Ichie Chima and Elder Nwokeji, Ichie Eziaha suspected that something was in the offing. He was an old-timer in matters relating to village property. He knew that the king's consent did not come this easy. For him to succumb to the whole thing just after a few meetings is an indication that something bad would follow.

The Freeborn Slaves.

"Can't we advise Dr. Erics to back off?" Ichie Eziaha said to Ichie Chima later on that day.

"The oath…" Chima reminded him.

"But…" Eziaha wanted to add.

"No buts, my dear," Ichie Chima cut him short, "Let his Chi fight for him."

They knew that the kings and all the *Ntisa* crusaders saw every Osu as a slave whose backs were meant for the Whiteman's canes, rods, loads, and never the comfort of a bamboo bed let alone the village land.

It was not long before their assertion was confirmed. It took little effort for the king to buy Agu over to his side. The two with Ekerue and Opanka started nocturnal visits to the other chiefs who were either on the king's side or undecided.

Soon they won many converts and got the number they wanted. It was difficult for them to choose a strategy but they eventually settled with the option of appearing to support Dr. Erics's agenda.

But Chima was not deceived by all the pretenses and so also was Eziaha. They felt very pained and miserable at their incapacitation. They wished they could alert Dr. Erics about the evil lurking behind the teeth the king and his cohorts bared before him, but the oath would not allow them. Chima had the guts to ignore the consequence of the oath but his

The Freeborn Slaves.

wife and children had begged him to consider them before taking his decision.

At last, Dr. Erics was given one of the evil forests near the Iyieti River. The Ajo-Ohia and the adjoining Ahihia-Ngwu forests where the Osu and the '*Ogbanje*' had their graveyard were all part of the land given to him.

The Freeborn Slaves.

Chapter 14.

The evil and the spiritual inclinations associated with the forests did not deter Dr. Erics and his compatriots. He would always say that people would know that good things can come from Ogbodu. He went about his dream project with ultimate dedication. In the end, what he achieved was an eternal *Ulondu* as he had named the hospital. No one in the village had seen, none had heard, and neither had it entered their village minds what magnificence meant until Dr. Erics built his hospital.

The place housed his family, his staff quarters, a borehole, and almost anything that could be needed in a mini general hospital. The sweetest thing about it was the equipment in the hospital. The village never knew there was anything like generating set until he brought his. It was a wonder they could not comprehend.

Dr. Erics had really made money in his career. Within a space of three and a half years, the hospital was already functioning. He had doctors from Kano, Port-Harcourt, Enugu, Lagos, and some African cities like Accra Ghana where his first son Okwuruoha who was baptized as Lui was going to school. Soon, the whole place was bubbling with life.

He could have built the hospital in any other place, but he had a binding mandate with his personal god- Chi to continue the struggle for his people's emancipation, thus he

The Freeborn Slaves.

believed that one of the best ways to achieve that was to bring development to the two-in-one village; "Charity begins at home" he had said. He believed the development would unite and make the people see things differently. Jealousy is a bad disease of the mind and a tyrant. It subjects its captives to a stranglehold twisting of the mind until it has bred a stench of needless hatred against a champion of a good course. The king's royal family who had pocketed the village and had always lorded it over the villagers since creation would not allow that. A low class had gotten rich and was becoming popular and that was a 'taboo' they just couldn't accept.

By now, Doctor Erics had employed some of the Ogbodu people as cleaners, auxiliary nurse trainees, and other types of engagements and most of them lived in the large expanse of the hospital premises enjoying a kind of life they never imagined existed. These were outside the people he had sent to school in the next village who equally dwelled on the premises during holidays.

There was visible peace and harmony in the New Ogbodu Village and it really scared the royal family. They felt that their significance was being threatened. Even the invaders who always came from the neighboring villages to molest the Ogbodu women unhindered had momentarily stopped as they all were part of the people treated at the hospital. All these were already distasteful to the royal council and yet they were still aware that the doctor was planning to build a school within the premises which he had turned into a kind

The Freeborn Slaves.

of brand new village as well. To worsen and further fuel the hatred of the king for the philanthropist, their own Owere children salivate and desire the goodies at Ogbodu and all could see it.

The presence of the hospital attracted other developments to the hospital villa. The Orie market became a bigger market there. The people cured in the hospital would see one business opportunity or the other and stay behind afterward and everywhere just kept opening up for the better. It was indeed wonderful to see how a single man's vision and the synergy of like minds were able to transform a section of a village into a mini-paradise. This made the king hate him and everything around him with passion. He was embittered that the credit and the praise were not to him but to some Osu.

On the other hand, the turnout and fall out of the hospital really made Dr. Erics feel a kind of fulfilled but then- he was busy feeling fulfilled while his adversaries, the devil's advocates busied themselves boiling superheated water for him. Even his efforts to bring in some children from the Owere clan were rebuffed and outlawed. As it were, yje king- Igwe Ogbuzulu and his cohorts badly regretted ever letting Dr. Erics succeed even this once. "How could we allow an Osu to become this popular?" they questioned in regret, "He is gradually taking over our village from us and we better tackle it now o!"

The Freeborn Slaves.

The Freeborn Slaves.

Chapter 15.

Just seven years of opening the hospital, the devil struck. Yhe kimg- Igwe Ogbuzulu had allowed himself some patience to let Dr. Erics finish all he planned and feel secured and free. By this time, Chima had died after a mysterious night sleep. His death left only a few men on the list of the villagers whose integrity still stood. They were the only people who challenge the king each time he raised his creed of "never let an Osu to be this popular". On one such occasion, Chima had threatened to report the matter to the police in the city that the village was planning to kill somebody.

"I would rather face the consequence of that useless oath!" he had fumed and stormed out of the palace. He had heard a voice which told him that Ezechitoke created no one inferior or superior to the other. God is one and had created all people equal before him and in fact uses the weak to shame the strong. This revelation really excited him.

The king had simply smiled as Chima threatened fire and brimstone. "a child should not lift his father up..." he had said halfway and stopped in a wicked smile before continuing, "Go away!" he shouted after him. Early the next morning, bitter wailing was heard from Chima's house.

Chief Chima was dead but the other palace chiefs all knew better. They knew the cause of his death but it only added to their fears and tears. They knew the truth but their own truth

The Freeborn Slaves.

could not set them free; they dared not resign from the cabinet due to the innumerable oaths.

....

The Igwe surreptitiously lured the Ndi-Oha into yet another oath and they unwittingly agreed and sold the village lands at Ngworogwu which they had in contention with the Okaome village and thus secured their support. The corrupt chiefs and elders got fat shares from the sale proceeds and their consciences were mortgaged. With the crump from the proceeds, they hired the never-do-wells and riff-raffs from the neighboring villages to carry out their evil plans. Those were the hit men of their birds of a-feather allies who always helped them to perpetrate and perpetuate evil.

"The okra plant is about to become taller than the planter," the emissaries would inform the kings of the villages whose support they sought. "The insignificant is trying to become significant and unwittingly trying to make something out of nothingness. Our slaves are outnumbering us and outsmarting us. Look at our land! The aliens are on the move to overrun and take over the rights of the indigenes- the true-borns! Impossible! It never happened in the days of our ancestors and it won't happen in our own time. The half-born can never and should never take the place of a full-born. Our king- Igwe Ogbuzulu, the elders, and the royal council of our land have come to you with tears in our eyes to help us curb this anomaly. Yes! It is an anomaly because the slave should serve and not served. He should answer and not call.

The Freeborn Slaves.

He should praise and not praised! These are the reason we are here" they usually finished.

The kings of the partnering communities were equally birds of a feather. They had always helped each other in village wars and this time needn't ask questions since it was a case of a slave and his master. They all had the tradition of stocking riff-raffs whose minds they corrupt with drugs, alcohol, ill doctrines and oaths of allegiance until all they knew and believed was the creed of master and zombies who do the bidding of their masters- the kings.

....

Hatred is the fruit of jealousy and haters cross boundaries to gratify their hearts' cravings.

One night in January, the daredevils blocked every footpath and way into and out of the hospital villa. Dr. Erics had believed that all was well thus there were no fences and it afforded easy access into the place for the hoodlums- they would have gained entry into the villa anyway. The inhabitants of the Hospital Village awoke amidst sleepy-confusion to behold a midnight invasion. They had gone to sleep when the hoodlums struck and ceased most of the people within the estate- Dr. Erics' family, the staff, and every inhabitant they could capture and set all ablaze. Like locusts and greenery, they voraciously ravaged, maimed and destroyed anything in sight both animate and inanimate.

The Freeborn Slaves.

Only a few people managed to escape from the invaders. They did not just escape from the villa; they equally bailed out of the Ogbodu village. Later on, with the help of the new indefatigable Rev. Father Gohill, the matter was reported to the police in the city. When the police came a few days later, the king, some chiefs, and some of the elders were taken to the headquarters in the city for questioning. They denied the entire allegation of having a hand in the operation and rather claimed it could be a mob action by some unknown angry youths who came from an unknown place. He too pledged to investigate it and bring to justice whatever community that had committed "such a heinous crime against my kingdom" as he had put it. "And this happened just when I was beginning to enjoy the contribution of this my my my em em em illustrious em em em slave, sorry, son" the king stammered as he faked a cry.

"You are the king remember?" the people consoled him, "And you shouldn't be doing this in public. Crying? No!" For lack of evidence, they were released to their family later on.

Chapter 16.

When Lui came home later on a holiday, he couldn't believe his ears nor his eyes or even the choking smell of carbon-monoxide-filled air in his nose. There was no *Ulondu* or the Hospital Village anymore and he just couldn't comprehend it. Everywhere has been destroyed and flattened. The whole place has been replaced with the dirty black smoke of destruction and ruin. He saw Amacha his father's friend but Amacha turned his face as though he did not recognize his friend's son. Lucky for him, his new position as the eldest in his family had moved him back to the Ogbodu village before the onslaught.

Amacha had said that his friend Erics contributed to his own downfall by not keeping and guarding his manhood until it put some rather willing women in the family way, and he couldn't summon the courage to go marry them even though he had given them his promise and thus they cursed him. He said Erics confided in him that he could not believe he impregnated two women at a time. He said Erics also confessed that one of the women had put it to him that since he did not want her to live in the future of his dream by leaving her that way, he too would not live in whatever future he dreamt of.

All these got Lui so shocked and devastated beyond words. He ran to Pa Anyaoha, his uncle's house, and the man started crying as soon as he saw him. "Come with me immediately," Anyaoha advised Lui and Kofi his father's friend who had

The Freeborn Slaves.

come with him from Ghana. They followed him without further questioning and found themselves at the Rev Fr. Gohill's house. There, everything that needed to be told was told and all they could do was cry. Fr. Gohill Bread on his own was like the only remnant of his church which had comprised of few Ogbodu people and many strangers. Many converts had settled at the hospital estate and some of them went down with the destruction while the remainders had all hurriedly left the village.

"Crying won't help you or change anything," they urged Lui and Kofi who seemed inconsolable. "What you would do for us is to remain here with Rev Fr Bread," Pa Anyaoha had cautioned.

"The evil people did not know that your father had a survivor. You shall remain here until we know what next to do." Fr. Gohill Bread chipped in. All Lui and Kofi could do was stare into the empty space sprawling before them.

Alone later on, Lui knew better than to stay in the village. He had better find his way out of the village before what killed his father and his people came for him. "Walls have ears" he had thought as he went through all that he was told. "They may have seen me enter the village," he said to himself. Out of fear and for his safety, Lui ran away in the night from Fr. Gohill Bread's house with Kofi. They dropped a note for Fr. Bread informing him not to worry about them and that they would be fine.

The Freeborn Slaves.

Chapter 17.

In Lagos, all entreaties by Kofi for Lui to follow him back to Ghana proved abortive. He had been so shocked and rocked that all he wanted was his pound of flesh. Lui stayed behind in Lagos leaving Kofi to wonder what a little boy of his age could and would be doing all alone in a strange and character-remolding land of the stars like Lagos.

The environment has a great quota to contribute to the character of an individual. Within ten years in Lagos, Lui had become the lord of a mafia. Having been forcefully rendered pocketless and hopeless the very first night of his stay in Lagos, he ensured he survived at all costs, and that made him rise so quickly to head an evil gang that specialized in many vices. The make-up of a man is not in his looks or size; it is within. Thus Lui was a small boy in some sense but he was heading men twice his age.

On his first night in Lagos, after Kofi had gone back to Ghana, some area boys had accosted him under the bridge where he slept and demanded he pay them rent for making an abode out of under the bridge. He had thought it was a little joke as he had simply told them he had nothing on him. It dawned on him where he had entered when without much ado, the area boys stripped him of his clothes; collected his little bag; bit him to a stupor, and went away with his belongings unhindered and unperturbed. His mentality changed immediately. He had believed it was the same Osu haters of his village or their associates that attacked him. His

The Freeborn Slaves.

mentality became so strong and wrong that even his gang members often wondered whether he was actually human.

As the days went by, he planned his age-page revenge. He never told anybody what went on in his mind or the story of his life. Then suddenly one night, as they jollied in their abode La Medina which he later bought over, he narrated briefly the ordeals of his life. He told them that he was ready for revenge and that he needed their support. It became a little wonder to them why he had been so mean a man. They felt sorry for him and wondered why he had kept it such a secret.

"Why did you not tell us since?" some of them asked.

"We should have trashed this thing and crashed all the people involved," Okpoka, their gang member had said.

"Nooo, don't you worry my guy," Ojiogwu supported, "we are always on time"

"What if the so-called king has died?" Okpoka queried,

"And it'd have been good for the king to bear the brunt himself," they agreed.

The Freeborn Slaves.

Chapter 18.

The Owere village and her people were dead asleep. Even their dogs and gods were all asleep too, and this became an eye-opener that even when in peace, still stay alert. Eternal vigilance is the price for peace and freedom. Nobody had any premonition of a fight even between ants let alone a reprisal attack on the village. The village had always been one-tracked legislation where the king and his council dictated while the Osu and others followed without much qualms or questions.

The Avengers came very late in the night, more than a dozen of them, and took the village and the villagers by storm. They seized the night watchmen they could find and their wooden rods and killed them all. They went to the houses of the Village Monitors which the Owere placed among the Ogbodu people and slaughtered them all. Then, they proceeded to the palace where they caught the first three guards sleeping. It was one of them who helped them to locate his colleagues in their hideouts.

They took all of them to the '*Obi*' and shot into the air. This awoke every other person who was still sleeping. They were all assembled in the '*Obi*' and advised to keep mute in their own interest. The sight of the guns they carried scared the dead night out of them all. The sound of it would have remained a living nightmare if they had survived the night. It was very different from the hunters' Dane guns they were used to.

The Freeborn Slaves.

The vengeance-takers first shot at the king's legs and ordered him to sit on the bare floor. "Evil begets evil," they told him. They asked for Obiechi the heir and were told he was away to Umuohia, his mother's village. In anger, they shot Ijeoma, the king's new and pregnant queen. At this, the king fainted but Lui and the gang continued their intermittent shooting unabated. This fetched the king's spirit from the land of the fainted and awoke him. He was weak from loss of blood and was begging for death. At intervals, they shot in the air to say, "We are still here."

"You would be alive to witness your death in bits," Lui assured the king.

"What have I done that you torment me like this?" the king questioned.

"You must tell me what my father Dr. Erics did to you first," Lui replied. It was then that the king began to really cry as the family realized what had hit them.

"It is good to see that the king cries too," Lui mocked him, "but I assure you that crying would not help you in any way just like it never helped your brothers- the Ogbodu people in your kingdom and all those innocent souls you wasted at the hospital village".

As this was going on, Major, another of the assassins got impatient again and shot two of the princesses and asked Lui to be fast so they could go and fetch Obiechi the son from Umuohia. He didn't know how far Umuohia was from

The Freeborn Slaves.

Owere village. He was only a stranger on a mission. They made sure everyone in the royal household was squeezed inside the palace and then set it ablaze. They watched it razed down and then left.

....

Egwuekwe was one of the night guards who survived the night of the rampage. In the nearby bush where they had hidden, he and his friend Egwuonwu had passed out severally each time the sound of the guns banged into the air.

After the operation, the undertakers chanted victory songs in Pidgin English. Even though the villagers did not understand what they were saying, they could hear the name of Dr. Erics being mentioned in the songs. The undertakers would have gone to Umuohia that night, but none knew the road and on a second thought, they decided to go. Before dawn, every villager had heard the tragedy that befell Owere people.

A fierce war broke out between Ogbodu and Owere. The Owere had agreed to exterminate the Ogbodu clan but surprisingly, the Ogbodu stood up to the occasion even with less significant weapons except for those provided by Lui and his gang- guns, machetes, rods, etc. Determination brings success and so Lui gingered his people to rise and fight and they did. Though the weapons had always resided at the Owere end of the village, the Owere people never expected what hit them. They were divided as some people were disenchanted since the refusal of the king to let them partake of the goodies Doctor Erics offered. Besides, there

The Freeborn Slaves.

are many ways to kill a rat, Lui and his people made do with what they had, and too, juju was not outlawed. He had expected this reaction from Owere people and so was already prepared before he declared his revenge mission. The Ogbodu people had waited for someone like Lui to rattle them to action thus they went into the war fully determined. They even toppled the Owere people's government but were soon deposed again after a few days before they could actually unfold their acclaimed plans of transformation. The Igwe Ogwugwu was the ally who really came to the rescue of Owere. His dynasty had remained a strong ally of the Owere village for generations after generations though not without a dear price for Owere. Momentarily, the chaser had turned to the chased but it only lasted a few days all thanks to the Igwe Ogwugwu who still brokered the truce for peace.

The Ogbodu people could not hide their joy over the intervention of Dr. Erics's family yet again in the life of the village. So many people were openly and proudly asserting that his family must be the chosen one for the salvation of the Ogbodu people.

Many people died in the war; more on the Ogbodu side though, but the Owere people equally lost some of their famous warriors. The two sides of the village were filled with empty homes of deceased war victims with weapons littering the compounds. In Owere, everyone feared for the life of Obiechi- the heir. Being an only son, he was not allowed to take part in the war and no one seemed to know his whereabouts. As Egwuekwe and Egwuonwu had

The Freeborn Slaves.

confirmed hearing the assassins asking for the heir that night, they all feared that they could come back for him. As the heir apparent and a king-to-be, he was supposed to lead the war, but this time, the heir could not be located and this also contributed to the loss the Owere village incurred during the war as some of the lower class people felt being used and never went to the war with full commitment.

The Freeborn Slaves.

Chapter 19.

Ekwueme Oboochi, Obiechi's maternal grandfather had to save his son. He took him to the Omajeta shrine at Opi village. He said that some detractors could inform the killers of his son's whereabouts and so he never told anyone where he took him. He even had a covenant with the priest of the Omajeta shrine not to disclose his visit to any third party.

There was horror, sorrow, and anguish all over Owere. The night of the rampage and the attendant war left the whole village in shambles. In Ogbodu's end of the village, there was untold joy. Yes, they lost some people, but they never had it so good. Even some of the settlers who hated the barbarism called caste in the two villages-in-one fought on the side of the Ogbodu people. They really made merry after the war such that one day, one poor man named Oturumbe, a man from Ogbodu, and his family had to devour a hen, her husband the cock, and even the eggs all in happiness. "If I die today" he had said, "my spirit would go rejoicing and dancing home to meet my ancestors". He was an active participant in the war and the coup. "What a sweet revenge!" he exclaimed, "What a sweet war! If not for Ogwugwu village, we would have annihilated them." He boasted; he was very happy. At least, they had made their marks and a kind of sounded a note of warning that Ogbodu were not just gutless or lilly-livered but could be the brave tiger whose tail no one should dare to touch. Even a goat pushed to the wall would eventually be really ready to do the fighting.

The Freeborn Slaves.

The Owere people were still battling with the horror and the sorrow, and trying to come to terms with all the unthinkable that had happened- the war, the coup, and worse still the missing heir, thus nobody even had time to notice the jollies going on at the Ogbodu end.

Chapter 20.

For more than three years, the Owere village did not have an Igwe- the king. The village was almost disintegrated if not for the palace council. In Owere land, it was customary for the son of a late king to succeed his father on the throne, but this time, their heir was on the run and nobody seemed to know where he was. Yes, nobody seemed to know the whereabouts of the heir because someone knew. Each time the matter came up or they wanted to move the crown to the nearest kinsman, Ekwueme Oboochi would claim that "My son is not dead and you must keep his crown for him".

After the kingless years, the fear had died down, and coupled with the trade in charms that Obiechi had learned at the Omajeta's shrine, he and his grandparents believed it was time to unleash the dragon. He had become impregnable, untouchable, unstoppable, insurmountable, and very ready for the throne.

On his day of coronation, he chose the name, Igwe Anunti the king of Owere kingdom implying that he was the deaf king who never hears and thus never fears. He held his fly-whisk in his right hand and his feather fan in the left. He made it clear that he was not afraid of any man. "This dynasty must continue!" he had blared, "And for the benefit of any doubts..., my kingdom still encompasses all the territories that my late father... yes... and my forefathers ruled; Ogbodu people and all they owned inclusive."

The Freeborn Slaves.

Praise singers and the people all hailed him as they sang and danced to his praises. "That's the king!" said one admirer, "My fearless king!"

"We must fight on to secure and own what is ours," he reiterated.

"Yaah!" the people chorused in agreement.

"The okra can never be taller than its planter" He asserted, "our property can never be stronger than us."

"Yeah!" they supported him.

"The Ogbodu as a village is only a part of our property and they shall forever remain so, after all, we believe that our forefathers bought them."

"*Iseeee!*" the people thundered in agreement.

"We can never be intimidated by anybody, never!" he fumed as he waved his fly-whisk around with the fury of a king who knows his onions and all was for his people's admiration.

"Unrighteous beginning is like the road to my anus," said the voice of Mogala the madman, "it only leads to an unrighteous smelly end". The people all turned round; some in bewilderment, others laughed at Mogala's admonishments which are usually seen as unhealthy for them because it was always an interspersed nonsense with some sense that pricks their consciences. "Yes, the hand that

The Freeborn Slaves.

goes to the anus must come out smelly. They say that peace is an expensive commodity that neither money nor power, not even arrogance can buy but still even Mogala will rest in peace," Mogala went on amidst the laughter of the madman that he was while Ashema the village provost brought him some more palm wine so he could drink and leave them in their peace.

"But what do you mean by all these?" Ashema comically asked as he handed Mogala more wine in the usual old plate he carried. "Yes," Mogala replied, "peace can never thrive in an atmosphere where there are imbalances, and where many still feel cheated and unappreciated. And those who wear clothes are still naked. The rain would be falling and I don't have the sun to shine on my roof- I can't understand," he finished.

"Mmm, Mogala, you've come again," the Ashema shuddered at the heaviness of the madman's words.

Don't mind him" the rest said to their own- the Ashema, "he is only a madman."

"Now you must go!" thundered the voice of Shinkafa the headhunter as he dragged Mogala out of the palace. "Who invited you here to advise us?" he fumed as he blew away the plate of wine from Mogala's hands and just then...

"Igwe Anunti 1," began the ***Onowu-*** the king's chief protocol officer sycophantically ignoring the fracas that had ensued between Mogala and Shinkafa, "you have spoken

The Freeborn Slaves.

well. Our traditions and kingdom and territories remain intact and there is no going back or going down on them" he urged him on.

"*Iseee*" agreed the drunken voices of the people in unison amidst mouthfuls of palm wine.

The Freeborn Slaves.

Chapter 21.

Lui. had become so hardened and unrepentant in crime after the revenge that his gang named him The Don.

"I feel so terribly bad to know that I have become a killer" he affirms each time he reminisces on his life. He could have made do with the rehab but there was none thus he drifted further and deeper into vice and engaged in all kinds of crimes. He was in and out of police cells and close to being convicted a couple of times, but each time he got behind bars, he never lasted more than a couple of weeks before his friends- partners in crime would grease some palms and get the case upturned.

He had friends in the army, the police, the press, the legal department, in fact, everywhere--evil has cousins. An uncurbed criminal tendency manifests itself in other crimes. He had become so notoriously popular that he even wondered whether it paid better to be a rogue. He was treated with a VIP reception in all the clubs and shows. After every successful robbery, oil bunkering, and drug deal, he doled out money and women to them as their own shares and dividends.

The Don made money no doubt irrespective of how he made it. He had dozens of people in his employ- the good, the bad, the ugly, and the mad. They included waiters, bouncers, and dancers in his night clubs, managers and agents in his casinos and brothels, oil and gas, and in the stock markets,

The Freeborn Slaves.

high-class prostitutes in his Booty-for-all Paradise to armed robbers and high-killers. He had become The Don of a mafia unofficially registered with the C.A.C. The government knew him and revered him. Some years ago, he was nominated for the award of Milkers of Our Nation (M.O.O.N) 'the MOON that thrives in darkness' as they love to call themselves, but he turned it down. They tried to make him see the goodies he stood to enjoy by joining politics; he would be shining in the dark since he would become the lone tree standing. "While many others wallow in penury, you would be the only one wallowing in wealth and the only messiah in sight- moon in the dark" they cajoled him. He would be free to use public funds to fund his personal engagements, transport money, and buy properties overseas and develop there, rather than waste it here trying to develop 'this undevelopable place' as they referred to the country; in fact, live as big as he wished.

When all that didn't make Lui change, they tried to advise him that "political power supersedes religious power, economic power, social power and what have you" they had told him, "and you could use it for vendettas whenever the need arises including against these ones who are always trying to put you behind bars."

They continued to cajole him but he refused to be swayed. None was able to know what he actually felt inside of him. When he looked at them, he saw a people so distant and detached from the true worth of a real human. For him, the only true human is he who knows the equality of every

The Freeborn Slaves.

human being. He felt sad each time he thought of how comfortably these fellows slept at night dreaming of love and romance while he had the stillness of the nights to dream only of freedom for his people and the whole of humanity. A world where everyone will be equal before the law and all will be judged as a human first before remembering his or her background. These ones go to their homes any time they want but for decades, he has been in exile just because of his fight to liberate his people. Besides, he felt he was morally unqualified. He knew that he became bad because of the village experience he had and the experience of his first night in Lagos when no one gave him a place to lay his head, and even the little belongings he came with were forcefully dispossessed of him. The experience was what shaped his judgment and made him see every other person as an enemy who held him, his origin, and everything about him to ridicule and scorn. He later got to know that even Lagos was originally developed by the synergy between the Lagos Aborigines and freedmen who settled at the nearest Lagos Island after slave abolition. Thus he wondered why his own people can't be one seeing how the strange bed-fellows of Lagos had been living in peace and harmony. He knew that no place, not even the places he was being advised to invest in is comprised of just one particular people, yet they have managed to live together as one.

Though decades later he realized how wrong he was about his perceptions and judgments and the resultant hatred, he had become so engrossed in crime that it was very difficult

The Freeborn Slaves.

to change. Besides, the patronage he got from the high and mighty never helped matters as it got even bigger. Some people called him "***Dike n'ubochi ogu***"- mighty man on the day of war" implying that on the day of trouble, people like him would be very handy. Others called him "***O kwuru o kaa***" implying that he stands taller than others. These names always blew up his ego each time and he truly relished them. His hotels and casinos supplied the powers that be with prostitutes, thugs, and human parts for their rituals during elections. Moreover, his lieutenants would not allow him to quit. He chose to remain faceless and nameless in the real scheme of things. "I don't have the moral conscience anymore to admonish or lead anyone let alone a people," he says to himself. His one bet with his personal God was the liberation of his people in Ogbodu. He would have to 'revolutionalize' their thinking and make them see that nobody was inferior to the other. Since that was his father's mandate, he saw it as his duty to complete what his father would have done if his life was not cut short. He has to free the generality of the two-in-one village from the mental slavery of superiority and inferiority complexes. He was not very good with religious things but he believed that God could never have made anyone inferior to the other.

Since there was no way he could identify who was and who was not an Osu, he had chosen to see every other person as a hater of an Osu and dared not take any nonsense from anyone.

The Freeborn Slaves.

The dream of freedom for his people was important to him but the reckless rascal life he led no longer gave him the time and zest he needed to bring it to reality. It had remained a tall dream for him. He had trained himself to actually be able to achieve his dream but what remained now was actually actualizing it. He and his people had reached the promised land of freedom of his mind's fantasy world while he was still sitting right in his room fantasizing, drinking, and smoking his life away. "Thinking is good, but doing is much better" he mocks himself.

Each time he sat in his bar thinking about the struggle, he would remember how much money he had stashed in the banks and even right under his roof. He would realize how futile his efforts were in trying to think that something somehow could make him forfeit them. Somehow too, his attention would just centre on his bar. He would behold all the brandies, Italian, Spanish, and all brands of wines that adorn the place and he would shake his head resignedly. He would fantasize about a glass of it in his hand and a sweet buxom lady caressing his hairy broad chest amidst encomiums from hangers-on and smile dryly. "Meeeehn, life is such a good thing" he would think, "and I can't forfeit all these just now." With this, he would sit back and reschedule his target to strike till the next year and the next year never finished.

The lion is a very brave animal but only if it conquers its fears, thus it dares to take on even animals twice its size. Contrarily, Lui, The Don had become so scared and couldn't

The Freeborn Slaves.

overcome his fears and that became his greatest undoing. He had the clout but not the courage. He had become so afraid of death that he couldn't even go home again to his village. Fear is a thief of courage and time. Lack of courage made him become a very loyal member of the *juju* shrines and equally knitted him into an ardent procrastinator. He had become so committed to his patronage of *juju* and charms that every step he had to take was dictated and directed by his *juju* priests and their charms.

Chapter 22.

The Don loved to live as he pleased. He was a rough rugged ruffian. He was the mean man who loved to look sad and lonely- the kind that no one wants to mess with. Before going out every morning, he studied himself in the mirror and then frowned some more. He smiled only when he caressed his brandy or his women who loved crashing into his embrace or probably too when he thought of his money. The smiles never lasted beyond before he does it with the women though. He gives money but never loves thus many a brokenhearted girl is one who wants more than money from The Don.

One night, he was drunk and slept with two women and impregnated them both. This surprised even him. He was already forty-four years old but yet to have a wife or a child of his own.

Some time ago he had complained to one of his associates about his "wifelessness" and the resultant childlessness, but this was not the way he had planned to achieve it. He was afraid of getting a child that would end up like him- a wicked weakling who abandons his course midway in pursuit of shadows. But still, he had some dubious excuses to give for his failure. He hid under the pretense that he was still carrying the royal blood and was just fighting his own people. When the two girls came the same day to complain about the same thing, it was a big surprise. The two girls

The Freeborn Slaves.

came, each on her own, oblivious of the other's reason for coming.

Jennifer was the first to come. She had told The Don how she had missed her period after the last time they stayed together. According to him, a prostitute never goes back to complain of being impregnated so The Don just tapped himself to keep cool and watch what the 'little' girl would be up to. She had said it in such a tongue-in-cheek manner fearing that The Don might get offended and flare up. She herself couldn't fathom what gave her such courage and impetus to confront The Don in the first place. The Don accepted responsibility for the unborn child if it actually belonged to him. Jenny assured him of her honesty and left.

Just as Jenny was leaving, Lucy came in and repeated the same story. She was the same girl Lui had slept with alongside Jenny that same night. It was a surprise though how The Don managed to recognize them. Maybe some things are just meant to be. He hardly had time or cared to know much about the girls he slept with but this case is different and he was quick to note that. He smiled to himself. He had guessed a foul play there and vowed to beat them to it. Equally, he accepted responsibility for the unborn child but still warned against anybody trying to impose another man's child on him. Lucy equally pledged her honesty and The Don gave her the same appointment he had given to Jenny.

The Freeborn Slaves.

In his usual manner, The Don would have gone to the appointment with at least two of his men but this time he chose to go alone. The men would just haul the girls into the booth of his car if they failed to prove their cases beyond a reasonable doubt.

Jenny as well as Lucy were surprised to meet each other this third time without knowing why. "Was it just coincidence or was The Don up to something?" they wondered. The surprise was written all over their faces and The Don didn't fail to notice that. He was surprised too that the girls didn't know why they were called.

"Why if I may ask" The Don began, "are you amateurs playing games with the master? I won't go asking you both to repeat what you told me but…"

The girls looked at each other realizing for the first time that they had come for the same reason. Surprised is just the only word that can describe what they felt but it was the extreme case of surprise.

"Which of you" he went on, "could convince me that I impregnated the two of you all in one night?" None of the girls spoke. Each was lost in confusion and disbelief and The Don noticed that too.

Jenny was the first to speak and it was only to defend the truthfulness of her claim that The Don got her pregnant. She affirmed that she did not know the other girl from Adam and that they had both met there these three times by mere

The Freeborn Slaves.

coincidence. Both girls said the same thing but The Don was not fully convinced. But now, however, he was caught up in an inner fear that only he knew about. He was battling to conceal the fear occasioned by a recall of his father's experience as narrated by Amacha. He didn't want to fall the same victim as his father yet he could not trust the ladies. He knew that the pregnant Jenny and Lucy were whores and could have been made pregnant by any of their numerous customers. As such, he took them to his friend The Dynamic Doctor at Ikeja for a DNA test and to find out if it were possible for him to impregnate two women all in one night. This was his hospital where he was treated each time he sustained bullet wounds those days.

The Dynamic Dr. Obyno confirmed The Don was the father of the unborn babies and so he was overjoyed when the two women gave birth to their babies the same day. Lucy was the first to deliver a baby girl in the morning and Jenny of a baby boy in the evening. The girl was called BigGirl and the boy he called BigChild. The Don proposed a four-year marriage contract to both of the ladies and they accepted. He promised to make them happy and he did.

Now sadly, just two years into the marriage, Lucy died in a ghastly motor accident. She was returning from the market when the brake of their vehicle failed and plunged into a stationary tanker. Many things went down in flames; cars, people, and the properties around. When the fire service men came, it was almost late. Some people were saved including Lucy but the fire had done great damage to her and after a

The Freeborn Slaves.

few hours, she gave up her ghost in the hospital. That was how Jenny became the mother of the two children and The Don later made her his permanent wife.

The Freeborn Slaves.

Chapter 23.

The family was living happily except for one thing. All the years, Jenny never saw any brother or sister or even a relative coming to visit their home. She knew The Don and his businesses but "even the devil has relatives" she wondered. She never heard Lui talk about his family, kinsmen, village, or town and this disturbed her a great deal. She had pestered him for centuries all to no avail. She had been living in the shadows and she didn't like it. To her surprise, he was never offended by how she worried him all the years. Many times she had threatened to leave their matrimonial home if The Don failed to deflate her doubts but those threats never moved him. Nevertheless, he kept assuring her that one day they would go home, but that she should be prepared not to run. This only heightened the fears she already had.

"It is now my twenty years of marriage with you," Jenny had said one night midway into dinner, "yet I can't say a thing about you. What's the meaning of it all?" she had queried for the umpteenth time. "What promise would take such long years to be fulfilled?"

"Dreams come true my dear," was all The Don said just like always. Jenny knew her husband was a mean man no doubt, but it still baffled her, what manner of a man that would not divulge the flimsiest secret even at the height of any ecstasy. To make matters worse, The Don refused to make babies after the "BigKids." "Who knows what these ones would turn out to be," he often wondered.

The Freeborn Slaves.

Even Jenny's mother was so upset with the situation that they all began to fear that The Don could be one of the fairytale ghosts that marry human beings in Lagos.

The twosome of BigChild and BigGirl were equally worried and they all had been pressing for the truth behind the mystery to no avail. The matter got worse when one day as they pestered The Don for an answer, he laughed hysterically and told them that even if he was a ghost, there was nothing they could do about it to change. "You are all my blood- ghost or human," he had said, "so you better accept what you cannot change". This had put the greatest fear in all of them even BigChild.

"No wonder this bad blood in us," BigChild said to BigGirl later on

"I have been wondering as well," replied BigGirl, "There are things I do myself and afterward wonder whether I actually did them."

"Yes, it beats my imagination and comprehension too," put BigChild.

Back in his days at the university, BigChild was the leader- Capon as they called him, of the notorious RBF (Red-Black Fox). Although his father did not tell him why he should not join, he warned him never to belong to any fraternity, but he still went ahead to be a member. On the other hand, BigGirl was not a member of any known cult. She was a Lone Lady

The Freeborn Slaves.

Gang (DLG for Double L G) as she preferred to be called then. She was never to be intimidated.

All the year, the two Capons tried to find the link to their root. They could not succeed. One because their names could not suggest the part of the East they came from. They were of the Igbo stock no doubts, but which part of the East. Besides, their surname was Lui and that did not suggest anything to them. They called their father all sorts of names each time he was at home but he remained unperturbed.

One day after his trip to God-knows-where, he came home and met the three of Jenny and her children standing at the entrance gate to their Thompson Estate home in Ajahi. He instantly knew what was up. They told him that the only ticket of access into the house was a revelation of his true identity. "Kill us all if you will," Jenny had said, "but that would be the only time you would get past us."

"Yes!" chorused the children, "Over our dead bodies!"

All entreaties by The Don to let him enter his home met stone-cold resistance.

"I have been doing this" The Don began, "to shield you from the dangers that await you at home but…"

"No!" BigGirl shouted, "Don't shield us anymore, we want to die."

The Freeborn Slaves.

"You are getting to seventy," Jenny cut in, "what becomes of us if something happens to you?"

"Ah!" the Don began, "are you wishing me dead?"

"See it anyhow you choose to but today is the end of the mystery," they assured him.

He made to go back and enter the car but they held his clothes and threatened to shred everything to pieces. The drivers and servants all stood in awe. They had never seen the sort of affront playing out before them.

"Today is the end of the mystery," said BigGirl and Jenny simultaneously.

"Okay," The Don said, "let's go inside, and I..."

"No!" BigChild interrupted, "Start telling us now."

After much drama and the threesome were still adamant and unwilling to compromise their resolve, The Don let the cat out of the bag in a normal Ogbodu dialect that sounded so strange to his family.

They were all surprised but still, they pitied him when they realized the genesis of his mean heartlessness. They were shocked to know that such inhuman maltreatment really existed anywhere in the world. They couldn't believe the event of the Black Night. "At such a tender age?" they all wondered.

The Freeborn Slaves.

"A wise child kills what killed his father before what killed his father kills him." The Don boasted. The story had made them realize the enormity of the atrocious taboo The Don had committed but they still longed to visit their home. East to West, North to South, home is always the best. They can't continue to live as fugitives forever. Now that they know their origin, the hunger surprisingly grew stronger. Moreover, they believed that after all these long years, the Owere people would have forgotten all the past and moved on with their lives, but The Don told them that the Owere people were hard to forgive especially when an Osu killed a freeborn son or daughter of the soil.

"Whoever became the king then must have died," Jenny opined.

"But I am still alive and I was there," Pa Lui reminded her and told them about the war and the coup.

"It was just like a family fighting itself," BigGirl said, "You are just a freeborn slave."

The Don looked at her and marveled. No one had ever said that to him before. Yes- a freeborn slave! To have that 'freeborn' something attached to his name really gladdened him. "But come to think of it," he said, "is there one who was not freely born? It is man's inhumanity to fellow man that sets the notion of freeborn and slave, upper class and lower class where the lower class has to pay tributes and tithes to the upper-class alias freeborn for being the beneficiaries of their collective patrimony and natural

The Freeborn Slaves.

resources." As The Don looked back through all the years, he realized that sadly truly everyone is a freeborn slave one way or the other and he too had grown up in a land filled with freeborn slaves; a land where those who work pay tithes and tributes through the racketeering "**Alayes**" the area boys to the idling godfathers. Drivers and commuters are always at the mercy of the big bosses or godfathers of those touts and have to pay for their sitting and drinking pleasures. While these racketeers harassed and maimed innocent citizens, the bosses sit down all day boasting away their lives in their dirty drunken voices on nothing noble at all but on infamous things such as how impregnable and impenetrable their charms and amulets have made them. He smiled wryly as he remembered how immensely he too benefited from such cronies and infamy. He was never a Yoruba man let alone an indigene of Lagos yet he bamboozled everyone and bulldozed his way to become one of the chiefs of the Central Extorsion Committee of the state. When some Owere people saw this feat by him, they concluded that truly, The Don was beyond them. The royal household and indeed the whole Owere people only waited for him to venture a return home.

Yes, for The Don, the city as well as the entire immediate horizon is all a place where although citizens see and believe themselves to be freeborns, they are indeed slaves. Their sweats are taken for granted and the fruits of their labor are forcefully taken in tolls and taxes by the financial gluttons who claim they work for the populace. The populace owns the bees and the honeycombs yet they have to buy their own

The Freeborn Slaves.

honey; their soil harbors the golds of this world, yet their homes are built with raffias.

"Maybe truly," Jenny said, "some are more equal than others or their heads are bigger than others."

"My village is a typical setting of the cruel politics world over. The poor who make up the lower class work hard and all they are required by law to do is pay levies to the ruling upper class, the elites who would never hear of, let alone let anyone from the lower class ascend or cross over the fence to the upper class. In my village, we all own the land equally. We have the same anatomy and physiology, sharing equal length of time a day with the same opportunity to till and farm the lands, yet the Ogbodu would only work for the Owere and remain a property to them."

"Every country is "unwrittenly" owned by some people," BigChild argued, "and it has always been that way where the poor have to work and still pay tribute to the rulers for legislating against them.

"Yes," The Don agreed, "and that explains the inhumanity going on for long in my village. The laws seem to be made only to serve the upper class and that's why we would still be here after all we did. I have benefited from this evil but my mission had been to gain from it in order to fight it." None could respond to what he said about 'what we did' but they all knew what he meant.

The Freeborn Slaves.

"But how did you know all these happenings in the village even whether the king is still alive or not when you never went home, or did you?" BigChild asked intentionally returning to the topic.

"Ah ah" began The Don, "I get all the information about what happens in my village."

"I shall forever treasure this day I heard you say 'my village'," Jenny said as she heaved a sigh of relief.

"There's nothing to hide anymore," Lui said.

"Yes, the mystery has been demystified," the two Biggies said simultaneously.

"And I can now have my peace?" asked The Don.

"And every one of us," they all agreed caressing the words.

"So you are not a ghost after all?" Jenny asked teasingly and The Don simply smiled. They have begun to see a new person in their father who smiles and discusses with his family. A new dawn in their family had come. They talked deep into the night and many other nights. The mystery had been demystified and they talked about it freely. Pa Lui in his happy moments would threaten to go back to his ghost world if they disturbed him.

The Freeborn Slaves.

"What if you had died?" BigGirl had asked one night, "We would have remained in the dark forever regarding our roots."

It was then The Don told them of how he had written everything down with the help of an expert and had submitted it alongside his will at the registry.

"Bag of secrets!" Jenny exclaimed, "One day one secret!"

"Daddy is really something else," BigChild agreed.

"It is really reassuring and refreshing to hear you call me daddy," Pa Lui said comically rubbing his hands on his tummy. "After all, I did all the things to shield you from the evil of fear and stigma that hunted and taunted me. I couldn't summon the courage to see you feel inferior to anybody, and I knew that once you become a killer, the stigma stays," he warned them.

They relish all the stories Pa Lui tells them these days but occasionally, there would be one or two that would spoil the whole story. One such story was that just like his father, Igwe Anunti also put another Osu girl in the family's way and refused to marry her. She was just one of the numerous girls with such experiences. The Owere people could use the Ogbodu girls for sexual gratification, and the boys together with the men for their farms and entertainment without batting an eyelid.

The Freeborn Slaves.

Now, the girl in question and one of the Igwe's wives eventually put to bed two look-alike-but-separated twins. The one born in the palace he called Ezenobi- 'King in Palace', and the one by the Osu was named Achuzie by his parents. The name Achuzie implied that in pursuing one to kill him, he may be pursued into his good destiny. The Ezenobi was in the USA.

"What of the other boy?" BigChild wondered.

"Just like your grandfather," The Don said, "was left on his own"

"Is there no police in that village?" BigGirl asked furiously.

"No, there are police in the nearby city," he replied, "but this has been the tradition of the land where the view of the Igwe and his council mostly counts. Everyone in Ogbodu has been praying to Ezechitoke for a messiah who will salvage the people's agony."

Every time they discussed their village issue, all could see how deeply hurt and vexed Pa Lui looked. He was usually unhappy that even the leadership of the Owere people which he still felt as belonging to had failed in their duties to the people. He saw them as playing bad politics like their likes everywhere who are only exploiting the people. They did not develop the village and all they did was cart away common wealth and transport it to the nearby cities for further development while their own village remained centuries

The Freeborn Slaves.

behind in development. They sacked the schools and yet they sent their own wards out to go get the same education. As a result, some sensible people had become apprehensive that some of the neighboring communities may soon be coming to trample on the Owere people since they no longer have strong force within them. There was division and insurgency among them and the only binding force for them was any matter that promoted caste and its creed. The Don always felt truly bad about this but he usually made it clear that he would not want any of his own to spearhead the liberation struggle again. The previous attempts their lineage had made did not achieve their aim.

"Whenever it pleases Ezechitoke our God," he always admonished, "He would send us a savior. My father tried and failed. I tried and here I am."

"You all tried in your own ways," BigChild tried to encourage his father.

"No, don't pacify me." Pa Lui The Don said, "Mine was even the worst. I left my fight halfway and never went back to it. I know that I… missed my ambition"

The Biggies didn't believe that God would throw down a messiah from the skies. They heard that Jesus Christ became a man before he saved mankind. They don't actually comprehend what that meant but at least they know the story. As such, they believe that a living being with flesh and blood must liberate the Ogbodu people.

The Freeborn Slaves.

They thought of going to the village alone without their parents but they didn't know the road. Moreover, they didn't know any of their relatives. They were all waiting for the next line of action to come out by itself when it actually did. Something happened that brought harmattan in June.

Chapter 24.

Chika was returning home from school at the next village for a midterm break. He was unaware of the masquerades that were performing. The Attama Akatapka had died and as a mark of honor and part of the burial rites, the Akatakpa masquerades had to perform. They have to accompany the deceased who happened to be their Chief Priest to the land of the spirits.

The people in the Ogbodu village knew about the occasion and remained inside, but Chika was unaware of it and came home. No sooner had he entered the Ama Owere than he began to hear the usual derogatory song *"Al'Owere anyi o"*

He was confused and transfixed because he was sure it was not the period of the year for the masquerade. Before he could explain to them that he was not aware of the occasion and that he never meant to desecrate their masquerades, they had seized him and his belongings he brought from the school.

"Shut up!" they shouted him down, "Who asked for your opinion? **Mtchew!**" they hissed, as they bit him. They took him to the Akatakpa masquerade shrine where they stripped him naked and then killed him to appease the Akatakpa spirit which they claimed he had desecrated. Afterward, they carried the corpse to his father's house, put it inside, and set everything ablaze. It was a quick dash to the nearby bush by the other members of his family that saved

The Freeborn Slaves.

them from being burnt alongside the sacrificed corpse. A minor feud broke out again but this time around though brief it was not sweet for the Ogbodu. When the news got to Pa Lui, he broke down in tears. Pa Lui really wished he could muster the courage to go home and fight. He couldn't let go of his past failures to dare try again.

"How could this still continue?" he queried. "This time in history and some people still won't let go of an archaic, barbaric, and despicable inhuman culture? What's this worthless faceless tradition of caste still doing in my village? Where are you, **Ezechitoke Ezechi Abiama** our God? Was anyone born to rule? Nooo! You never created one to be inferior to the other o, for if you did, that would have been most unfair of you"

He continued to pour questions to their creator. Though he got no answer, he believed he heard him right. The incident really saddened him and he couldn't hide his sorrow anymore.

His wife Jenny came in and saw her hubby in a very agonizing mood and was startled. It was never easy to extract information from The Don. He had always been a mean man and only spoke what he wanted others to hear. Even at over seventy years of age, he still oversaw his businesses. He believed he alone possessed the requisite experience. Since Jenny must talk to her husband somehow anyhow, she waited for a while and then went in again to enquire from him what was wrong. To her greatest and strangest surprise,

The Freeborn Slaves.

The Don broke down in tears. The two Biggies had come in just as Jenny was about to begin the conversation and met their father crying, for the very first time.

He told them the news concerning Chika and the masqueraders and how it had just rekindled all his wishes about the struggle for freedom. The major reason for his tears he said was his failure to achieve his mandate and the promise he made to his God and his father. He has been one freedom fighter exiled in the mountains in a foreign land. For decades he has been passing messages to his people at home to boost their morale to stand up and fight yet he himself had been too cowardly to start the fight. This thought like always saddened him but this time around, he openly confessed his wish to see the liberator for his people come before his life expires. He had plans, but he didn't have the willpower to back it up. Love for his wealth and women, the dubious belief that he was fighting his own father, and all sorts of confusion contributed to divert him from his course he said.

But then, just seeing their father's tears was enough to make the Biggies vow to avenge whatever brought the tears. None of them tried to stop their father from crying.

The Freeborn Slaves.

The Freeborn Slaves.

Chapter 25.

"Dad?" BigChild had started later on in the evening. The Don didn't say a word, he heard his son alright.

"You gave birth to me right?" BigChild went on.

"Yes," The Don answered.

"And you named me BigChild?"

"Yes," the Don answered again.

"I know you had a reason for that"

"Yes," was all Pa Lui kept replying.

"And you know that your blood runs in me?"

"Yes," again from The Don.

"Eventually you would wish me to take over from you if you died before me?"

"Yes."

"And you trust that I would fit in properly into your shoes?"

"Yes but..." he answered almost unwillingly this time. "You may fail just like me and maybe get consumed in the process and that's why I would no longer want you to follow my footsteps."

The Freeborn Slaves.

"But you are not a failure Daddy," BigGirl who had joined them put in.

"Oh yes, I am," The Don went on, "I am a failure. All the heartlessness and things I did began because I wanted to avenge my father's death and further his course. I thought money and toughness were all I needed so went on to get them. I went about training myself to be fearless and heartless all in a bid to do whatever I could to free my people and… impose our ideology- equality and equity on all of us the Owere people. Now, did I achieve it? You know the answer. Here I have been in exile for decades, yet my mission is unaccomplished. I got carried away by all sorts of rubbish reasons and even wealth and the friends I kept. This wealth you see here doesn't give me a single joy anymore, in fact, it contributed immensely to stray me away from my mission."

"But you taught me to be fearless, Dad, and to make money," BigChild reminded his father.

"Yes, but that was just to make you never believe that you are inferior to anybody. And even right now, I have come to believe that violence, money, and all that are not the solution we seek"

"Dad?" BigChild called, "You cannot achieve real peace without some measure of violence. It is the peaceful violence that pricks people's consciences that will compel everybody to respect everybody else's rights and you need

The Freeborn Slaves.

the cash to run around or play some politics and...," he stopped off the statement.

"Nooo! Hmmm," The Don chuckled, "As you see, mine never paid off well."

"Maybe because others did not fight with you or because you left your battle midway, and never went back to it again," put in BigGirl and they all laughed.

"No, they fought with me," The Don protested. "I told you about the war and even the coup, maybe because I left my mission halfway."

"Maybe the fight was not enough," BigGirl insisted.

"Hmmm," was all The Don could utter.

"Dad?" BigChild continued, "I am promising you that if you take us, in fact, if you take me to the village"- BigGirl cast him a 'you-selfish-sabo' kind of look and BigChild caught the gist and went on, "I shall reunite the two warring brothers without much of violence; just a piece of peaceful violence, it shall be the final part of all this" BigChild said enthusiastically. "See I've been playing around the matter, Dad, but I know the truth."

"The truth...? What truth?" The Don asked apprehensively. He was thinking that maybe his boy had found out another of his top secrets.

The Freeborn Slaves.

"You see, Dad, life is a mystery where a superior selfish force called destiny compels all to do its bidding and makes it impossible for one to determine what happens in his life." BigChild went on, "You all tried in your own ways but the truth is that anyone who gets involved in a venture is only a co-actor in an already written script. Some must begin the script while others join along the line while some others must conclude it. You must join wherever destiny calls you and exit at its appointed time. Another funny truth is that in the end, you find out that even those things you thought you did were not actually done by you- someone else did. No one acts in isolation or in a vacuum- you must act on something and with others. And you see, the real actors in a movie are those not seen. They work behind the scenes- the writers, directors, editors, lighters, costumiers, etc, and even the man who fumigates the forests in the make-believe. They are the ones who put together what is shown. This is the same with man and divinity."

They all marveled at what BigChild said including BigChild himself.

"Well said," The Don put in, "but what are we going to do?"

"Keep at it… working and let things work out themselves." BigGirl replied in support of her brother.

"Yes," BigChild agreed. "Yes," they all agreed, "Keep working at it."

The Freeborn Slaves.

"Dr. Erics Ifedili had the liberation of Ogbodu at heart and died because of it," Don Lui reflected, "I, Lui the *Okwuruoha* his son had it and became a killer for it. And now I am seeing the same spirit in my own children, who knows what their own fate will be? My father's era was lenient, mine was violent, maybe theirs is the salient part of this trident. Ha! Must it be my family?" he wondered almost aloud as the whole thought tired him out. "Let's see what happens next… and things must work themselves out," he agreed as he strolled up to his room.

The Freeborn Slaves.

Chapter 26.

"I am giving this matter a serious second thought," The Don confided to his wife later in the night much to her surprise. The Don seeking her opinion, hey, it was incredible!

"That would be great," she replied happily, "and we can't wait for the positive reply."

Jenny was openly happy with the development so far. She sang and danced for the first time in her marriage. At last, she was about to unravel the deepest mystery of a husband she had lived with all these decades. She too belongs to the Osu but theirs was not as severe as the one her husband had experienced and described to her. That much she knows. There was a time she traveled home to see her parents in the village and narrated the stories to her mother. She too confirmed that such things did happen in their village in the past but not this time anymore. Not that there had become a complete mixture between the 'real' villagers and the slaves, they still find it hard to intermarry, but at least no one claims ownership of the other. There seemed to be a superiority creed everywhere she had said.

BigChild suggested they use their father's influence with the police to go and meet the king and confess that he was sorry for the offense he committed decades ago. They would then, later on, he suggested, invite the government into the matter. The Don declined saying he wouldn't want to involve the

The Freeborn Slaves.

police in the matter knowing who they are. Maybe he was being selfish too knowing who he is and what he had done.

"Where were the police in this recent murder?" he queried. "The king and his cabinet just like all other ruling classes have enormous powers in the villages," he informed them.

"But the police are supposed to protect the people," BigChild said.

"Yes, but only when you invite them," the Don said, "and especially in a compromised faulty-foundation clime like Owere, it is the king's position in a case that matters most of the time. If he is displeased with you, he could easily see you as a leftist and label you a traitor."

"It is ridiculous!" Jenny fumed, "Arrant nonsense!"

"Besides," The Don went on, "Is it not the same police that I have been with and known all these years? They would lead you to the middle of the stream and forsake you."

"I have some friends in the army, and they would come into it if need be," BigGirl said.

"In fact, let me consult with my uncle Anyaoha first." The Don said.

"Who is Anyaoha?" they all questioned.

The Freeborn Slaves.

"Anyaoha is my father's brother," Pa Lui began, "He was a little boy living at Ibite Ogbodu when they killed my father. In fact, he is now old. He and his grandchildren had been taking care of our family house in the village"

"Do you mean we have a family house in the village?" they all especially Jenny questioned. The Biggies just looked on as they couldn't believe their ears.

"Yes now," replied The Don very casually, "I built a family house in the village."

"But you never went home, or did you?" she asked him surprised and yet expecting another surprise.

"No, I never went home but I sent money through people and somehow, he managed to build us a home there. They are all in the will."

"A will? Daddy, I know you still have loads of surprises for us," BigGirl teased.

"Even after death o," they all agreed.

"Daddy, I fear you the more," BigChild said not knowing what else to say.

"It was all for your safety," he assured them.

"But how come they have not destroyed it or are there other such mansions there?" BigGirl asked.

Tony Ik Odoh

The Freeborn Slaves.

"That's what I am saying," Pa Lui replied, "I know that the reason the evil royal family had not destroyed it is simply to lure me home."

....

Okenna just like many other Ogbodu people could not believe his ears when he got the news of The Don's proposed homecoming.

"It must be a serious joke," they all agreed.

"How could this be after several years of being in exile?"

"If I ever leave this god-forsaken village," said Chidi, Okenna's grandson, "I will never dream of coming back to it."

"Everybody is not as selfish as you," his grandmother, Okenna's wife cut in, "you would forget even your own parents and siblings just to be happy alone?"

"No!" he tried to deny.

"No, what?!" his grandmother rebuked him. "You can see, even while in exile, Uncle Lui still remembers his people at home and sends them money and several gifts, and this your selfish mouth has eaten from it."

"I'm sorry mama," he pleaded.

The Freeborn Slaves.

Everywhere had become calm as she admonished her grandson. The other kids all kept quiet and listened. "When things are going well for you and you are happy," she went on, "don't forget home and those who started with you and suffered with you, ok?"

"Yes grandma, *ezi nne*," he agreed.

The Freeborn Slaves.

The Freeborn Slaves.

Chapter 27.

News is like wildfire or the wind whose direction can hardly be controlled. In spite of the efforts to keep the news of Don Lui's proposed homecoming a secret among the elders of Ogbodu village, one elder told his wife during their midnight duties and the wife told the children and they told the other children and so on, and so forth until it became an open secret.

As the news soon went around the whole of Ogbodu village that Lui the philanthropist was coming home, people were filled with joy of expectation. They eagerly awaited their hero and philanthropist. Many who never actually believed in the story of a "Lui" who never comes home but builds roads and supports community projects, sends money to the indigents at home, and many others to school all waited to satisfy their curiosity. Even Anyaoha's children and grandchildren never believed him each time he gave them money and gifts he claimed to have come as their share from their uncle Lui who lived in god-knows-where. Even those years when he was building his own house and the The Don's mansion, they didn't believe him. Some even thought maybe he stole the money, but since he was always in his shade and never went out of the village and equally always slept in his house every other night, they didn't know what else to believe. He only hands them the money after their village meetings and when the children enquired from other children, they realized that they were not alone in the confusion.

The Freeborn Slaves.

As the Ogbodu people were expecting their man, the Owere people were also expecting him; the difference was in the reason for the expectations. Even though the king had become old, he was unhappily happy that Lui was coming back home while he still lived. He had spoken a binding oath of vengeance upon himself against Lui for committing such a heinous sacrilege. He had sworn to avenge his father's death by whatever means. There was a time he and his friends spent sleepless nights at the Ochete's shrine in the Okoharia forest where they chanted all sorts of incantations on Lui's real names. They invoked misery and death to visit him wherever he was all to no avail. It was never easy to deal with The Don spiritually. He had become a moving sanctuary. No wonder the royal family knew that he was in Lagos and they too visited Lagos, yet they could not send the royal assassins to kill him- "I've been there before you" he told anyone who dared him.

One night, the king- Igwe Anunti, and his friends continued their incantations as usual. They were calling on Lui to come and cook alongside the **'Okpa'** dough they were cooking upon which they enchanted their incantations. They wanted the fire from Ochete's shrine to visit Lui wherever he was that night and strike him dead. Suddenly as they were performing their ritual, his image disappeared from the mirror with which they were monitoring him. They became confused and were left wondering what went wrong. All of a sudden, a mighty hippo appeared from the blues and shattered and scattered all the things around them including

The Freeborn Slaves.

their altar, the sacrifice, and the fire, and promptly disappeared. That did not deter them at all. All they did was simply change to plan B. The chief priest began by rebuilding the altar. Afterward, he chanted a countless number of incantations round the arena, gathered pieces of his shattered mirror, spoke to the debris, and made the mirror whole again. They held their hands in agreement, chanted binding oaths of death upon anyone among them who would refuse to unite his body, mind, soul, and spirit with their prayer and soon the king- Igwe Anunti and his cohorts were on another round of cooking, dancing, chanting of incantations and calling on The Don's name.

"Lui Okwuruoha," the chief priest continued, "*ekwekwe ga-ekwe n'uta ekwere*"

"*Iseee*," they all chorused in agreement. Their prayer always ended this way.

As soon as they finished their prayer, they saw the form of a giant man approaching them from within the thick darkness. As the figure approached closer from the distance, it had a cigarette between his fingers and heavy smoke pouring out of his nostrils. The space around his face was as smoky as a chimney. Some were scared while others just looked on as they wondered whether it was a human or a ghost. While they looked on in confusion, the figure was now nearer and they recognized him immediately as Lui Okwuruoha's spirit man and promptly increased the tempo of their incantations and enchantments. They were overjoyed to see that their

The Freeborn Slaves.

prayer was quickly answered. They had succeeded in overpowering The Don's spirit and had brought him to their shrine.

Suddenly while they watched, the figure changed to a man, then changed to a housefly and flew towards them. At this, they all rose spontaneously and pursued it to catch it. As they chased it about in all directions to catch it and crush it, the fly flew into the nostrils of Onyeke, the Chief Priest of the Ochete deity. Quickly and instantly, Onyeke's head swelled up and before their very eyes, he fell down and died leaving them all scampering for safety out of the shrine. Afterward, Igwe Anunti and his advisers never went again for any spiritual battle against The Don.

Igwe Anunti, his council, and the Owere people had waited for this singular opportunity all his life for The Don to venture a return to the village, thus if the rumor was anything to go by, they too were ready for a final showdown. "Let him come," the king fumed as he moved unhappily on his chair during one of their cabinet meetings where The Don's matter was being discussed. Igwe Anunti the king may be old and weak for the real physical confrontation he had hoped for but he could best be described as an old weak freak, freaking out for revenge. He knew that there were many ways to kill a rat. He was ready to try his luck again and do whatever it took to accomplish this one dream, "After all, this is still my territory. Moreover, it would be the biggest shame and taboo for an Osu to kill a freeborn and still walk upon the sands of the village even after a hundred years in exile. I better get

The Freeborn Slaves.

consumed in it than live and see such a taboo. An Osu is still our property and must be made to pay the price due to a slave who killed his master. Yes! I must avenge this sacrilege and redeem my image."

It was a tough situation for the Igwe Anunti's camp as they planned his age-page revenge. Black or white, he must respect his oath of vengeance. Now too, The Don's mind was already made and there was no going back.

The Freeborn Slaves.

The Freeborn Slaves.

Chapter 28.

As the family moved to enter the car, The Don raised up his eyes and hands to the sky. Maybe he prayed. But that would be the very first time at least before his family. He looked at his family and sighed, looked at his children again, and smiled dryly. This made all and sundry very uncomfortable to the point that Jenny confessed resentment to their going home.

They had proposed to travel in two cars, but just as they were about to enter them, The Don changed his mind and ordered that they all travel in one instead.

This sudden change of mind about cars and the seeming prayer that he had offered earlier made Jenny very nervous and instantly she felt the need to empty her bowels at the toilet. She suddenly began to regret ever pioneering the agitation for the village visit. She had barely recovered from all this when an unknown weird-looking man showed up as their driver and this promptly sent her back to the toilet.

They had many drivers but just the day before now, The Don settled them handsomely and sent them packing. Now they have a young oldie as their driver. BigChild could have driven the car, so they all wondered why the strange behaviors. Maybe the stranger had been inside the room with The Don because none of them saw him when he came. Maybe it was after consulting with him that their Dad

The Freeborn Slaves.

changed his mind about the cars. Maybe he was a co-villager. So many maybes.

"Are you sure this man is not about to waste all of us for disturbing his life?" BigGirl said to BigChild.

"Whatever," he replied, "is it not better than living without knowing who you truly are?"

"Does it mean that all the stories were just make-believe- mere fabrications?" she went on.

"Whatever," he replied, "for me, I am prepared to find the meaning of all this."

"I am beginning to feel that we should have waited for things to unfold by themselves," BigGirl said, revealing her failing courage.

"And continue to live in the dark about who you are?" BigChild asked, "No! It is when you push a certain button that you trigger an implosive chain reaction that would send elements of the mysteries crashing into the content of their within for a revelation. Ignore your fears and you will concentrate on your courage for success."

"Well said, but I am still afraid that Daddy may be up to something." She said, "And if these stories Daddy has been telling us are all lies, then nothing is impossible."

"Maybe D   addy is a ghost o," BigChild was saying, "but we shouldn't fear. We have pushed a button and

The Freeborn Slaves.

an implosion would occur. Let's be ready for the debris that would fly around."

"How I wish Biggy... that we would be alive to tell stories of this debris." Jenny reflected.

"On my part, I would be alive o; I don't know about you," BigChild said.

As they were about to enter the car in which they were to travel, it dawned on them that Abo doubled as the driver and the witch doctor. This really scared the early morning breeze out of Jenny and her children.

"If I had my way," Jenny said aloud now, "I would say let's cancel this journey! Ah ah! What's all this? Let's live our lives, please. I'm getting more confused and frightened by the minutes"

"You won't understand," Lui replied coolly but meanly too, "The coast is not clear at all."

"Then let's stop!" Jenny shouted, this time not caring how her voice sounded.

"We are going," the Biggies said simultaneously.

"Let me find out what each person's plans are," Abo said mischievously.

"I've told you that you won't do that to these children," Lui cut in.

The Freeborn Slaves.

"Are they more to you than they are to me?" the stranger asked The Don in a sternly raised voice and the family only continued to wonder who the stranger was.

"Is it not better we lay out our plans and... and..." Jenny stammered.

"He wants to hypnotize you," The Don threw in.

"Not me, not me," they all shouted and before you could know it, Jenny was already on the ground cursing everybody including herself for demanding this journey.

"It is not something to worry much about," The Don tried to pacify her, "and even if something happens, it is better I show you your roots and also prove that I am not a ghost. Hey... Lui Okwuruoha," he almost wept this time, "I have failed to live like the true Don. I have failed to live by my name *Okwuruoha*. I spoke only once and have been mute for decades... oh please forgive me."

The family was lost and confused as to the meaning of all that their father and husband was saying. They were so scared and afraid that none of them was able to ask for the meaning of it all. They had never heard him call his chieftaincy name before and to compound it all, he was asking an unknown being to forgive him.

After much ado, they set out homebound. As they entered the Benin-Ore expressway, it became clear to them that their father was not a ghost after all. They talked and

The Freeborn Slaves.

chatted like never before with The Don once more sheathing his color as The Don and trying all he could to make his family feel safe and secure and reassured. At the stopovers, in Ore, and Onitsha where they refreshed and refueled, The Don had met a countless number of associates and old friends who talked with him in low tones. As they traveled, Abo did them the favor of explaining the places to them even though nobody knew if he was from anywhere near. In fact, even The Don didn't seem to know where Abo hailed from. Abo had simply stormed on him one night and after telling him some secrets he thought no one knew, they had become friends. For an instant, they all seemed to forget all their worries. Some even slept.

When they got to Eha village, it was around six o'clock in the evening. Eha was the last village before Owere village. As soon as they entered the Eha village, Abo pulled over at the Chez Restaurant much to a delightful surprise of The Don. Chez Restaurant was the oldest cool corner in the area but remains very relevant in all generations. It remained a very sweet place to be in a typical village setting. The ownership kept changing from one generation to the other as the owners died and bequeathed their ownership to a successor.

The Don did not want prying eyes and wagging tongues to start so he believed too it was wise for them to cool off and wait for time.

The Freeborn Slaves.

It was around 8:30 p.m. when he thought it was safe for them to leave. He was not afraid though. He was only concerned about his family. As they made to enter their car, a thunderous heavy rain began unannounced.

While they waited yet again for the rain to stop, it was a kind of thinking galore for all. Pa Lui was brooding over what awaited them at the villa. BigChild was recalling all the stories The Don told them in recent times and he couldn't but wonder why such inhumanity and maltreatment were being meted out to his people. It was amazing to him what the driving force was. For an instant too, he wondered why he was so concerned and bothered about people he had never known, seen, or interacted with. "Like father said," BigChild was thinking, "whenever a child is crying and continues to point to a particular direction, either his father or his mother is there. Yes, it's clear that my family had been chosen for this particular mission; to be the messiah… but they have all failed somehow from granny to daddy but I'm not going to fail. The time has come for the drama to be concluded and I will be or at least aid the protagonist," he assured himself. "What of Achuzie?" he suddenly asked.

This took The Don by surprise. Their thoughts were doing the same mathematics. He was only reminiscing on the plans he already had since ages ago and here now something tells him that his son was on the same thinking lane too. He was happy suddenly at this thought but he controlled himself- he was still The Don.

The Freeborn Slaves.

"He is there," The Don replied, "and why do you ask?"

"Nothing, just that my mind remembered him just now," BigChild lied. The Don heaved a sigh that somehow suggested he knew what went on in his son's mind and of which he was happy.

BigGirl had her plans too. She knows her way. She would leave the village immediately and go to the nearest police or army barracks and make one or two friends. She would arrange how to identify the killers who killed Chika. The soldiers would just storm the village one night and execute her plans. It would simply end up as a case of unknown soldiers and nobody would hold anybody responsible for anything. She would then pick it up with the king. "That wicked old fool," she cursed under her breath. She would be glad to make him pay with his old life for the so many deaths he and his lineage had ordered all these long years. Even if it means doing it in the full glare of the people and later paying with her own life, she would not mind. As she turned this thought over in her mind, she felt some bad-black blood rush to her eyes as it usually did whenever she was annoyed.

She was also happy to think of how the Ogbodu people would be happy at the end and how fondly she and her family would be remembered even after death. There won't be any freeborn-slave palavers anymore. She believed that her action would be able to put the strangest fear in all the

The Freeborn Slaves.

villagers such that the memory alone would be able to scare the devil out of even the strongest Osu hater in Owere.

"And after that," she thought almost aloud, "nobody would dare call anybody Osu again. Come on! No one is born to rule and the other to follow. There should be equal opportunity for all. In fact, by the time I'm through with them, they will see the famous Queen Amina of their own land." She heaved a sigh at this thought.

How she wished just now that she was married and had a son. It would have been sweet to imagine her son becoming the king of the two-in-one village, and then putting sanity into the brains of the entire villagers. "But maybe I wouldn't have had the guts I now have," she consoled herself, "As a wife and mother, I would have had to seek permission from my husband and kids before doing anything. It feels great too to be single after all," she realized happily.

"Oya o, let's go," Abo said cutting into everyone's thoughts just as the rain heaved a relief.

"Ogbodu my village," The Don called, "here we come."

They set off into the Toyota Sienna and off they went. It was around 11:00 pm and everywhere was dark when they got to the village. The rain had also fallen in their village as well. Just then Pa Lui remembered how difficult it would have been for them to cross the village without the night guards seeing them. "The chilling killing coldness of the weather

The Freeborn Slaves.

had chased the guards back to their homes to seek warmth by the sides of their wives," he had said aloud.

Abo was happy to assist his boss at the moment. The Don is his boss now because he is driving him and his family. The Don becomes his client and loyalist after this journey. Don Lui is a regular caller at Abo's mobile *Amusu*- witch temple where Abo is the chief celebrant. There, he dictates to The Don what to do and what not to do. Abo is a spiritualist, a spiritist, a hypnotist, a ritualist, an herbalist, an extremist, and every other 'manufacturable' bad word that ended with …ist, occultist inclusive. That was all the people could make of him.

Just at the Owere entrance, Abo abruptly stopped the car in the middle of darkness, a red ribbon in his left hand and a black one in his right. He spoke some strange languages, put the red ribbon between his lips, and moved in a roundabout fashion round the minibus like a sleepwalker. That was actually when it dawned on the threesome who actually had been driving them from Lagos.

Abo danced and shouted, shouted and cursed, cursed and cursed, and then he finally smiled. He then re-entered the car and put away the ribbons. "They have gone," he announced to the surprise of the voyagers and even Pa Lui as they all wondered who it was that 'had gone'.

He explained that an uncountable number of spirits were sent by Igwe Anunti the king to kill them all at the Owere entry

The Freeborn Slaves.

point. "But for my timely intervention," he continued, "you would all be dead now."

Pa Lui cast another worried look on his family, this time with a 'we would have stayed' kind of look on his face. Ordinarily, the look on his face should have put fear in the threesome, but this time, they have all become ready to face whatever confronts them.

"When there's fire on the mountain," BigChild began, "everyone chants 'run run run', but that shouldn't be," he stopped and looked at his people. "Yes," he went on, "we shouldn't all run. Some should be courageous enough to remain and put out the fire because down the valleys there may come flood and where would we run to if not to the mountains?"

"These words should be on the Mable of great quotes," reflected Don Lui proudly. "A hero can only beget a hero," he thought to himself, "but am I really a hero?"

Slightly before midnight, they got to their uncle's house. It surprised them that The Don could still recognize the roads although not much has changed in the land except for the gullies that had resulted from erosion.

"Thanks to this rain that chased the guards back to their wives' sides," The Don said again as they entered the compound.

The Freeborn Slaves.

"I was ready for them," Abo buoyantly assured him, "they wouldn't have seen or heard us pass them."

The Freeborn Slaves.

The Freeborn Slaves.

Chapter 29.

The returnees were to be taken to the Lui's mansion without delay. Anyaoha's grandchildren had cleaned the place up in readiness for their return. Besides, the place had been inhabited by free tenants who were just asked to leave some weeks ago. The returnees left immediately for the Lui's family house promising to come in the morning to see the rest members of the family. They were almost out of the compound when Adaku, Anyaoha's new wife woke up. His first wife had died some years ago thus both the grandchildren and children had to make him remarry and this time, to a much younger woman. They had all awaited the returnees but when it got late and they hadn't shown up, sleep won the battle and all others went back to their homes. She had never seen Pa Lui or any member of the entourage before. She welcomed them the best she could, considering that she just awoke from sleep, but it was written all over her face that she was happy, and had eagerly awaited them.

They drove through the small bushes and shrubs, down the valleys and gullies, and up the small rocky hills and cliffs until they got to the mansion. Even in the darkness, and with their experience of mansions in Lagos, they could make out the beauty of the houses.

"Thank you," Pa Lui said to his dear uncle. That was all he could say at the moment. He was so overwhelmed. The Don's house was built many years ago, yet it has stood the test of time and still remains modern even now. Anyaoha and

The Freeborn Slaves.

his children had made sure it remained clean and inhabitable by ensuring that people always resided there. For their return, the whole compound was cleared of any unwanted weeds and shrubs and repainted. Everywhere was just sparkling. The Owere royal family had sometimes indeed hoped to acquire it for themselves when they must have lured The Don home and wasted him.

"You deserve the best," Anyaoha replied in his cracking old voice, "but thanks all the same for the compliments. I'm glad you like it."

They did not bother to unpack their loads and luggage since it was already well past midnight. Besides, Anyaoha had assured them of his grandchildren's lending hand tomorrow.

They simply brought out their beddings which they brought from Uncle Anyaoha's house, and clothes for a change into their night dresses.

Jenny was the happiest for so many reasons. She had finally allayed her fears that her husband of many years could be a ghost. For an instant, she had confessed her love for the village. She specifically treasured the peace and serenity of the village night filled with the melodious cries of insects and little creatures. The crocking sounds of the praying mantis, frogs, and toads. The occasional near-human cry of some creature they called Bushbaby all combined to give the village night a sweet melody. The fresh smell of the wet red earth filled their nostrils complimenting the chilling and refreshing cold breeze across the starless sky to give them a

The Freeborn Slaves.

feel of what real coldness means. They really were going to enjoy their stay here they thought.

"But it's just these evil people who would not allow one to have a breathing peace here," Jenny sighed resignedly.

The Biggies were already in a room trying to fix the beds and the bedding. They had all become so famished with sleep heavy in their eyes and heads.

While they did that, Jenny was savoring the flavor of having dismantled the object of her fear all these years, just as Pa Lui got ready to see his uncle off.

"So you are not a ghost after all?" Jenny said enthusiastically. She could wait no longer before saying it out. The Don only acknowledged it with a smile.

"Bring my torch," Don Lui called to BigChild just as he set out with his uncle.

"This night Dad?" BigChild asked. He was already lying down on the bed half-made heavy with sleep.

"Yes please... ***k'eji oku ele ehihie*-** is torchlight meant for daytime?" he asked.

BigChild brought the torch and joined his Dad and Abo in seeing uncle Anyaoha off.

The Freeborn Slaves.

The Freeborn Slaves.

Chapter 30.

The Don and his uncle had walked just a little distance when he asked them to go back and have their rest while he went home alone. They had just turned back having agreed on that when Uncle Anyaoha made one last sound and that was that. His head had been separated from his body, and everywhere had turned into pandemonium and disarray. From all corners, the fire was flying in and burning everywhere, from the sitting room to the bedrooms and indeed everywhere. There were so many voices singing victory songs. Those were from the hands that had ambushed them.

The hoodlums had agreed to let them sleep before setting them ablaze so that they would die peacefully, but a last-minute change of decision by Ngwodongwo the killer-in-chief changed the situation.

Before one could say hey, or Abo could chant his incantations, Pa Lui was already out of sight. He was nowhere to be found- he had disappeared. As the commotion ravaged suddenly, untold fear had ceased the Don but fear or no fear, if you do anyhow you see anyhow. Out of fear, he mistakenly touched his navel without first chanting his incantation and thus incurred the wrath of the gods. Only he, Abo, and Akaria the great Dibia knew what to expect as a consequence. Akaria was an outcast from an unknown clime who practiced high voodoos, witchcraft, and magic. The Don did the disallowed and the allowed consequence surfaced.

Tony Ik Odoh

The Freeborn Slaves.

During his days with the Juju men, he had vowed that no mortal was to see his corpse. The Juju man had warned him of the enormous and dangerous consequences of such a bold step, and he agreed to live by it. Akaria the great dibia agreed with him and gave him the charm he sought but warned him that there were places around his navel which he should always beware when touching. He was made to know that there lay his power to appear and disappear thus he must be very careful never to touch the area by mistake, or out of fear as there were certain incantations he must chant before touching it. He used the power to hide from the police during his bad-boy days though the government equally knew many other ways to kill such a rat like The Don thus they always caught up with him when they needed his money. Too, there is time for everything and at the appointed time, his charms failed. The Don had touched the tiger's tail whilst riding on its back, and coincidentally the tiger was hungry, and angry at that same time, thus the meat of his body quenched the wild cat's hunger.

As quickly as he touched his navel, so quickly did he also pay the price- he exited the land of mortals. In a land where rude arrogant men compete with proud inconsiderate gods, such words as 'mistakes' do not exist.

However, as he disappeared in fear, he collided and got trapped in the giant *Akpu* tree nearby, and all they could hear was the sound of his shrill voice as he shrieked, and begged for mercy. Maybe Abo would have tried to help him then, but he had to save BigChild, and maybe too, his skills would probably have been useless, and amounted to nothing against the giant of spirits in the *Akpu* which makes it the giant of all trees in the world.

The Freeborn Slaves.

Now, as The Don disappeared, some of the hoodlums were scared beyond words and took to their heels without looking back. Those were the lily-livered ones who were not very prepared for such a high class mission. Others remained resolute to bring their mission to a logical conclusion. They went home and came back more fortified. They enchanted some incantations unto the giant tree and moved towards it in order to pull it down but some unseen forces blew the first one backward and away from the tree, flung another against a nearby Iroko tree, and struck another down with a great thud leaving him sprawling and writhing in pains. Afterward, they sprang up and all fled for dear lives.

Back in the house, Jenny was already burning on top of the bed set up a few minutes ago. BigGirl was being led to the Toyota Sienna which was already enraged with fire to be burnt alive.

They were taken by such a rude shocking surprise that they couldn't put up a single fight. Even when Abo came to, his incantations yielded nothing on the hoodlums who had gone the extra mile to prepare for it. They had equally made sure they drummed it into the ears of the Osu that they were not mates. A freeborn is always superior in everything so they bragged.

In a twinkle amidst the burning and killings, Abo and BigChild saw a young man standing akimbo on the other side. He pointed at BigChild and told his men something; maybe he wanted BigChild alive and that was when Abo knew the urgency of his duty call to save BigChild.

The Freeborn Slaves.

Chapter 31.

To their surprise, Abo and BigChild found themselves at the Okoharia Forest. Abo had held BigChild and said something that made them disappear but surely it was not at the Okoharia Forest that he planned to land.

In the world of the spirits, Abo had erred by not recognizing the territorial spirits that guarded the Owere village. Even amidst his own confusion, the priest of Okoharia Forest Deity had a field day mocking Abo for thinking that his poor wit could outwit that of Okoharia the god of wisdom and power.

"You should have sought permission from us and the gods of the land before embarking on this journey," the priest of Okoharia lambasted Abo.

"Shut up, young man, before you incur wraths too big for your head!" Abo shouted the old priest down and this really scared as well as surprised BigChild and the priest and his servants. "Do you know how villages and their gods are founded?" Abo queried harshly.

"How could someone call an oldie like the priest of Okoharia a young man?" BigChild wondered.

"You say only what you know and what your head can carry!" Abo warned in red furious eyes.

The Attama had to at least pretend that he was not scared, thus he went on- "No one knows why the two of you were spared but your charms had been rendered powerless and impotent right from the moment you pursued our spirits back at the Ama-Owere."

The Freeborn Slaves.

"Ah!" BigChild shouted in utter bewilderment. He would never have believed it that Abo did anything at the Ama-Owere if another had told him.

"For you," the priest went on referring to BigChild, "I am told to let you go. Oh, you think we didn't see you coming?" Attama queried BigChild.

"Then what happens to to to…" BigChild was saying but stopped short. He wanted to ask what fate awaited his companion even though he didn't know why it bothered him.

"Hmmm as fo... fo... for this one," the priest stammered while hiding his face from the mystic Abo, "I don't know what awaits him. I have never seen such an inexplicable young oldie with no spiritual history. I have tried in vain all along to ascertain his spiritual biography."

"Now, are you done?" Abo snapped but got no reply.

Suddenly Abo began to play on the priest's intelligence. He appeared in the priest's mind and pretended to be thinking and to be vividly confused. He appeared to be wondering why all that had to be true. He knew he actually broke the rule of territorial authority, "but I have paid some dues to that effect and I wonder why I was still unable to disappear," he appeared to be thinking.

"You were able to disappear?" Attama happily cut into his thoughts, "Because of this young man here and so also that you may go and tell the truth about the infallible powers of our gods. Again because you are probably just a businessman." The priest had become happy that he was beginning to get into the spiritual biography of the mystic seated before him.

The Freeborn Slaves.

....

Adaku, Anyaoha's wife, and the entire Ogbodu village were awoken by the victory songs of the assassins as they went back to the Igwe's palace.

They immediately knew the reason.

"The king killed the returnees," they all concluded.

Adaku made to run to Lui's house for her husband but a giant stopped her and ordered her to go back home.

"Have you killed them?" she enquired. "What of my husband?" she went on even as the man refused to talk to her. "You better kill me as well you murderer," she cried and held onto the giant.

The man dragged Adaku back to her house and, "Remain here!" was the stern order he thundered in a very hoarse voice: "You would carry the corpse in the morning," he finalized and left.

On hearing this, Adaku fainted. The children were all awake now and wailed uncontrollably.

"When will this stop?" they queried the air before them but there was none to reply to them.

The Freeborn Slaves.

Chapter 32.

Back in Lagos, Abo didn't enter into The Don's house.

"You are all alone and very much on your own," he had said to BigChild while holding his shoulders, "be very careful and never lose guard," he advised.

BigChild just stared into the empty space before him while Abo gave his advice. He was totally lost as to the meaning of all that had happened. It was so incomprehensible to him why such a fairytale could be true in his life.

"Is Ogbodu filled with a people so incredibly insignificant and worthless not to merit a second's thought by God about sending them a savior?" BigChild cried, "Maybe it is true that some are divinely made to be slaves to others. Otherwise, why should all this happen? How could one explain why generation after generation, some people are allowed to trample on and dehumanize others for nothing and yet they succeed all the time?"

"Take it easy," Abo cut in, "That's the irony of life but there is always a reason for every season, though hidden now it must surface later in the future. I shall see you some other time."

"You are the only person…" for a split second before BigChild could finish his statement, Abo had doubled himself the way a wall shimmers, crossed his hands across his chest and that was that; he had vanished. This scared the life out of BigChild. When he recovered, he recalled that a few days ago when they set out for the journey, none of them saw Abo enter the compound.

The Freeborn Slaves.

"Fake! Fake! Fake!" BigChild cursed. "How could you possess all these powers and yet couldn't save my family?" This grossly angered him and he fumed and cursed himself for not teaching the cheat a bitter lesson.

"He must have promised my father protection before we embarked on that ill-fated journey," he reasoned. "I must be the biggest fool not to remember this all the while I have been with him. Now he is nowhere to be found after misleading my entire family to an untimely grave. Or did he charm me? This is a cruel world, but… am I any better?" he queried himself. "But I acted in ignorance," he was crying uncontrollably now.

"Forget the past," he seemed to hear a voice tell him, "and concentrate on the future."

"How can I?" he harshly replied the voice of his mind.

He thought of how they had all set out for a journey just a few days ago, five of them, and now only him.

"It is really unbelievable," he agreed. It baffled him what he was still doing staying alive. "All alone? In this whole place? In this whole wide and wild world?" he kept asking. He hurried off into his room upstairs. His mind was already made on what should become his fate too- to end it all.

"Which Busi…?" he shouted at the voice which seemed to have asked what would become of the father's business if he killed himself.

The Freeborn Slaves.

"Then, the freedom struggle?" the voice in his mind came again, "Don't be a coward."

He was fed up with life no doubt but this last question and statement made him quiet even to his very surprise.

"The struggle? A coward? No!" he shouted. "This dream is already a killer dream sent from the pit of darkness. I will have nothing to do with it again, oh no!" he was sobbing uncontrollably.

"Life is a bluntly sharp paradox, young man?" the voice said, "Dreams come true boy, and achievers never give up on their dreams."

He didn't know why but he heaved a sigh of relief at the statement and found himself feeling better, though he still didn't know what to do. He didn't know the road to the village, and neither did he know a single person there. The uncle that he even saw was already a victim of the monster called freedom struggle.

He remembered that some decades ago, his father The Don was in the same dilemma, but never ran away. The Don had equally said that the spirit of their ancestor who had appeared to them had instructed them to be strong and liberate themselves.

"But he didn't actualize his dream and… must it be my family?" he queried.

"Now listen" the voice of his mind began, "Like our faces are different, so are our destinies and missions here, and like you said some time ago- 'you are simply a co-actor…'. Be assured that the fire given to the child does not

The Freeborn Slaves.

burn him unless the child decides to let it. And again, nobody sends the child to sell salt in the market and send the rain against him. He who sent the child to catch '*Nkakwu*', the poisonous rat, would equally provide him water to wash his hands afterward. And more importantly, where there is a will, there is a way."

Too many questions with so many frustrations and no solutions flooded his mind. He argued with himself back and forth until sleep ran away from his eyes. The madness that could result from sleeplessness was another worry that crept into his mind.

"I would simply enjoy myself..." he reasoned, "then... than... than waste my time and energy carrying the burden of the whole Ogbodu or whatever it is called on my little head. I... I... I don't even know them. Let things work themselves out men. After all, even my father said no one knows how Owere and Ogbodu and this caste system began. They all met it like that." he finished and like magic, his eyelids became so heavy with sleep and he slept off.

And truly, no one seems to actually know who Owere their acclaimed progenitor actually was as they had different versions of who he was and how he came. One had it that Owere the progenitor of the Owere clan was the wealthiest man of his time. He owned vast farmlands and many livestocks and plantations. He even had fish farms in the far away Adada River. At a very tender age, he had become richer than anyone in his village of Umuokpu and was revered by all. He championed many courses that benefited the Umuokpu as a whole.

The Freeborn Slaves.

At a time, there was a war between the Umuokpu and their neighboring village, the Ajobodo. It was Owere's wealth that made the Umuokpu victorious in the war. The Umuokpu village had a scanty population then and thus their neighbors always trampled upon their rights.

When their enemies came again to molest them, he encouraged his people to stand their ground and fight back. He used his wealth to secure support from other friendly neighboring villages that joined them to fight their enemies. After the war, he came back with him countless number of slaves and items he got from the spoil and he was unanimously proclaimed king of the Umuokpu to replace the king who had died in the war without an heir.

Afterward, he moved further westwards of the Umuokpu village to the present location where he settled with his wives, children, slaves, amulets, ammunition, and property. There he built and fortified his kingdom from where he administered the whole village which had been renamed Owere. He led them all in peace- slave and freeborn alike, calling them all his children.

After his death, there arose a dispute over the sharing of his properties. As the disharmony lingered, those from the freeborn wives who were fortunate to be the older ones united against the ones born of the slaves. They had access to the weapon with which the king had safeguarded the kingdom, thus they drove the slaves and all that related to them even those from the entire Umuokpu to a place they

The Freeborn Slaves.

referred to as Ogbodu- meaning something like an inside-turned-out cloth. The west end of the village contained many of the evil forests and used to be the place where the aborigines threw away the Ogbanje children and also sacrificed the slaves to the gods. However, they lived in peace in their respective camps since each was given a measure of the king's wealth.

Then a time came with a king named Ntisa- a descendant of Owere who refused to know how the people of Ogbodu originated. All he cared for was that they were slaves of slave mothers and fathers and must be seen and treated as such. He joined them all together in one community and called them Ogbodu.

Though the slave descendants of Owere had grown in number, major political and military powers of the kingdom remained with the Owere people who were still in control of the kingdom.

This king- Igwe Ntisa reversed all the peace the two villages had enjoyed. He proclaimed Ogbodu and all that reside there as the property of the Owere people. He subdued them under his military powers and gave laws that determined what would become of Ogbodu and her people. He introduced the *Osuimi-* village Monitors whom he placed in all the different clans of Ogbodu village. Their duty in Ogbodu was specific and direct. They were saddled with the responsibility of identifying, collating, and reporting anything whatsoever that was not in favor of the Owere people to him.

The Freeborn Slaves.

Each time he bought his own slaves he sent them to Ogbodu where he had the shrines for the different gods he worshipped.

After Ntisa, subsequent kings took after him since they now utilized the manpower of the slaves in their farms and females for their sexual gratification.

Even the waters of the rivers, a natural gift became a rare gift meant for the exclusive use of the freeborn Owere people.

Yet another version said Owere was a strong Dibia from Burute village. A certain Nkwoegbu village was running short of male children after they stole a prince from their neighboring village and used him as a sacrifice to appease their god who had demanded the blood of a close prince. The prince before breathing his last had reminded them of all the support and friendship his father had shown them. He cursed them and their land for choosing to pay good with evil and the curse followed the village of Nkwoegbu severely. Now the village contracted Owere the Great Dibia to come and help them cleanse their land after they have suffered for decades. The last male child of the village was already above forty years yet no cry of a newborn male is heard anywhere in the village.

Now, Owere had done all that was required of him and within the next nine months, there were numerous newborn male children in almost every family of the Nkwoegbu village. The village invited him in order to appreciate him for a job well done and for him to consolidate his work. Just

The Freeborn Slaves.

before the night of his final ritual, a certain little boy came to his room. Owere gave him food and a piece of fish. As the boy was eating, he informed Owere of a plot by the village to assassinate him so as to render his charm indissoluble. Owere pretended as though he was not interested and played it down. As the village heads gathered together in the night for the final rites, he ordered them to prepare the fireplace for the cooking of ***Okpa*** dough. He purposely brought their attention to his ***Oji-*** rattling iron staff, by asking for it and then he pinned it on the ground near the fireplace. He began to chant his songs and dance around the fire as he was cooking the dough and invited all to join him. He directed that all should sit immediately they hear him shout "Faam!" as that would signal the end of the rites and the completeness and indissolubility of all he had done. On hearing this, the ***Ndi-Ogbuishi-*** killers who were hired for the job started getting ready and taking their positions beside him. Their mission was to cut off his head as soon as he shouted the "faam!" command. They all joined him in singing and urging the ***Okpa*** dough to cook quickly. As he was singing, he was talking in parables about a people the devil had vowed to destroy. He said the people were on the verge of being rescued from drowning, but instead of cooperating with their rescuer, they pushed their rescuer away and rather tied a millstone over their necks. As he spoke his parables he watched with his eyes the movements around him but feigned ignorant. The people caught his drift and coincidentally, as the assassins were trying to reach an agreement on whether to strike immediately or not, the

The Freeborn Slaves.

dough was ready, and "Faam!" came the command from Owere. There was confusion everywhere. The fireplace has been scattered and the dough spattered everywhere. The fire too has been extinguished and the splinters and sparks spread everywhere. As some sat in obedience to the Dibia's command of "faam!", others scampered for safety while the *Ndi-Ogbuishi* went for their target to do their job. But then, there was no Dibia anymore; Owere had vamoosed. As they looked, they saw him flying away in a shooting star. As soon as he shouted his "Faam!" command which stood for the sound of the extinguishing fire, he grabbed his rattling iron staff, and off he went in a shooting star. He flew and flew but then he realized there was a problem- he had lost his routes. He could no longer locate his village. Soon, he got exhausted from flying and landed in an unknown land engulfed in wars. With his powers, he won victory for them and later on, forcefully united the warring parties as one village. He renamed them Owere and became their king. He led them in peace though, and called all of them his children. Later on, he invited all his fellow Dibias, siblings, and friends from his Burute village who came and joined him. They then divided the villages and peoples among themselves and fashioned how to administer them. Then the people became angry about how the aliens were treating them and their resources. As they continued to advance in their invasion and quest to dominate the entire immediate horizon, they met another group of invaders at the upper side of the village. There were conflicts and an imminent war. It was at this point that they decided and agreed that since none

The Freeborn Slaves.

of the lands belonged to any of them, then, rather than kill themselves over it, they should rather fashion out a way to jointly conquer and administer them and then share the loot. That was how they conquered all the different people and their kings and took over all their lands and assets. They suspended all the ways of life of the different people and united them in their own way.

After many years, various villages that had similar experiences as Owere villagers began to revolt. Some of the people in Ogbodu part of Owere and other villages had become angry over Owere's and his ilk's domination. When the revolts became increasingly unabating, the mother of Owere who also rules Burute village convoked an assembly of Great Dibias and Witches where they discussed the issue.

Now, Owere attended the General Assembly of Great Dibias and Witches where it was agreed that no longer would any Dibia or village have dominion over another. Foreign domination was banned and outlawed. Many years later, even when others had left, Owere refused to go and this led to a force by the people to oust him. He was angry that he had to go, and thus before he left, he ensured that those he and his military met on the upper side who were also the side that gave him the least resistance to conquer became the king and resided at the place he called Owere. He relocated all his weapons of war and arsenals to the Owere end of the village and advised them to always hold on to power if they hoped to remain relevant. He made them believe they were born to be masters over others. He promised to always be with them

The Freeborn Slaves.

and to support them. While he was leaving, some of his children whose mothers came from the Owere village refused to go with him preferring to remain in Owere village. From them came one of his descendants Ntisa and his crusaders. They later united the villages again by force and labeled the Ogbodu side the Osu. It had remained so in the minds of the people that even centuries of generations ago have come to believe that Ogbodu people are slaves and they have continued to fight for their freedom.

Many believed the first version because at a time when the dehumanization became very unbearable a total stranger believed to be the spirit of the dead Owere began to appear to his people both at Owere and at Ogbodu. He warned the Owere kings to remember that they all descended from him and thus ought to live as one people. He consoled the Ogbodu people and exhorted them to be strong. He told them that a time whenever they become strong and think, they would free themselves from the shackles of their servitude. Yet others believe the second version since the Owere side has continued to receive military and other support from Burute village centuries after Owere had gone back there as against the Ogbodu side who though had been crying for help never received even a listening ear.

The Freeborn Slaves.

The Freeborn Slaves.

Chapter 33.

Every thought always desires to return to its abode- the mind. BigChild must have slept for ages and when he woke up, he felt refreshed and renewed. Nevertheless, he had a tough time chasing away the same thought that sent him to sleep.

Out of frustration, he resorted to his old normal lifestyle and started smoking away most of his time and partying. He was usually at every other big boy's social gathering. Some managers of his father's businesses understood him. Others mocked him and wished him dead too. They scoffed that ill-gotten wealth always ended in the hands of spoilt children who knew next to nothing about what to do with them. Some others even wanted to run away with The Don's money but were promptly stopped by Abo even without BigChild's knowledge.

Now, BigChild had always loved social life but this time around, he was not feeling happy at all with the kind of life he was living even though it was not different from his usual life and he didn't know why.

"Life, what do you want from me?!" he shouted at himself one early morning after partying all night and now battling a near migraine kind of headache from the hangover.

"It's all in you," he heard right inside his head.

The Freeborn Slaves.

"I am tired and confused!" he shouted even louder and soon he was snoring. As soon as he awoke, the first thing that greeted him was the thought of his father's business- the very first time since all that had happened. "Life must go on after all," he said to himself.

He started attending to the businesses. Many had thought that without The Don, the businesses would die with him since he rarely allowed anyone near his businesses. But when BigChild started asking relevant questions, many were surprised at how informed he was about the businesses. The people had thought The Don to be a mean man but they truly saw a meaner man in his son, the BigChild. Even BigChild himself never knew he learned anything from his years at the university, thus he was surprised at his own bright performance with his father's businesses. He was as prudent as he was mean and non-compromising. Many of The Don's associates marveled at this and agreed that a lion can only beget a lion. They really loved BigChild and wished he would take his rightful position as a replacement for his father in their clubs. Yet in the midst of the encomiums and his engrossment in the desire to take the business to a new greater height, his mind always said to him that he had an even greater task ahead- the freedom of his people, the Ogbodu people.

A few months into his new life, Abo knocked on BigChild's door.

The Freeborn Slaves.

"Have you come again, you deceptive baldhead?" BigChild fumed rising from his seat to go grab the juju man. "You deceived and stole my family from me, eh?" Suddenly, he just changed his mind abruptly and went back to his seat.

"I know what you have been through," Abo began, "but believe me, I never meant to deceive your father. I am sorry," Abo apologized.

"Just thank your stars I'm already in a good mood."

"Yes I know," Abo agreed.

"What do you know?" BigChild snapped, "Don't even start because I won't believe you."

"I've been watching you and I realized you are ready to live life again," Abo said ignoring the mockery by BigChild. "You see, I was the only true friend, your father, The Don, ever kept and…"

"And you led him to that shameful death, huh?" BigChild cut into his speech.

"You would not understand what happened there," Abo said, "and I won't even try to explain them to you."

"There's nothing to explain to anybody, you em em em… *mchtew*," BigChild hissed. "My father, my family is gone and that's all you wanted."

The Freeborn Slaves.

"I have not come to defend myself or explain anything rather I came to thank you for deciding to move on."

BigChild simply looked at him and hissed.

"Now let me reveal some truths to you," Abo began, "When a child falls, he rallies up to continue the race, but when an elder fall, he gets up and looks round to identify what he stumbled over. There are three things that drag a man down- women, money, and power. The first two have pulled your fathers down and the third is in your hands. The contents of your father's wrong life would make for a very long moonlight tale for children thus he was dropped from the plan. Looking at your antecedents, I don't think you would fare any better seeing how inclined to rule you are. The choice to give you another chance has been made though since you have yet stuck to some important instruction and never shed innocent blood. You are the kingmaker, power-drunk, and unyielding, a focused achiever! But then, Oughtn't you to remember to know when to quit?"

This left BigChild wondering whether the last statement was a statement or a question and whether it referred to something that would happen in the future, now, or in the past. Abo's lecture, prophecy, or whatever it can be called was all to the consternation and terror of BigChild who had become increasingly confused as to the true identity of the mystic discussing with him.

"But who are you?" BigChild asked apologetically.

The Freeborn Slaves.

"That's unnecessary!" Abo snapped, "Just listen, you have not thought of the things your father submitted at the registry," the juju man went on getting BigChild even more confused.

"Of what use would that be again?" queried BigChild, "Everybody is dead now," he finished resignedly with his lips quivering in fear.

"Please just get it," pleaded Abo, and with that, he bid BigChild bye. Abo had become BigChild's greatest companion and revealed to him that the Don was still in that tree and could be consulted.

Later on, BigChild and their lawyer went to the registry to get the will and what he found in the will baffled him.

"I never knew my dad was this careful," marveled BigChild, "How my thoughts just rhymed with his."

"That was his strength," Abo said, "and it made everybody to be loyal to him."

The Freeborn Slaves.

Chapter 34.

A good teacher once said: Subtract sentiment from a situation and add selfless heartlessness, the answer is a tough decision that yields good results. That was the central message Don Lui wrote in his plans of how he hoped to achieve his mandate; freedom for his people. BigChild was ready to use it. His father had trained him for a rainy day like the one here.

....

It was raining heavily at about 8:45 p.m. BigChild had just made up his mind and called KE. For a few months that seemed like an eternity, the two had neither seen nor spoken to each other. After the day at the Booty4All Paradise, KE was receiving pay from the outfit without doing any job. All efforts to even set eyes on BigChild failed, and besides, he was warned that his job specification didn't require him to come anywhere near the 'paradise'. As the bad boy he was, he didn't bother his head much about that.

"It's BigChild," he had begun, "Can I see you tomorrow at the Obollo Road Club?"

"Sure," replied KE over the phone.

"You bad o," KE accused BigChild.

"Not to worry," BigChild assured him, "stuffs are ready to be trashed."

The Freeborn Slaves.

"Sure?" shouted KE, "I've waited for like ages, no voice, no eyes of you men!"

"We talk tomorrow," BigChild said.

"Should I come ready?" KE asked.

"Not on the phone, man, tomorrow, 7 p.m. at Lapelle Obollo Road Club," shouted BigChild and then he let the line go dead. "Come however you choose to," he murmured to himself.

At 7 p.m., both men were seated under the guava tree hidden from view. They were not drinking anything. After sealing their deal, it was time to toast to it and they did.

The Freeborn Slaves.

Chapter 35.

Early morning of the agreed date, around 2:00 a.m. on Monday, February 10, it was an Orie day, the market day as usual. Ezenobi was sound asleep after a long journey. He had just returned from a long trip to the USA. Abo had informed BigChild that Eze would be coming home.

Ezenobi could have flown by air but he chose to travel by road. He wanted to behold the beauty of the roads he read much about in the papers. The Lagos-Benin Expressway especially at Ore town had been fixed and now bubbling with street lights, flowers, and trees along the walkways. He equally wanted to savor the beauty of the latest transformation that has taken place- The Asaba International Airport- the best in the world. He had read that the Rivers Niger and Benue had been dredged and world-class Riverports built at Onitsha and Lokoja. He wanted to behold the revamped railway lines that at some point ran side by side with the new expressway. At the stopovers, he hoped to see the terminals of one of the ultra-modern underground metros for fast trains which now run from street to street and even lead to the revamped coal mines and deep forest farms. Before he boarded the Osinachi Marcpolo bus, his eyelids had trembled in anticipation of the good sights and pleasure-filled journey home.

What a bitter-sweet journey he had. Yes, those beauties were all there- right there in the papers! However, after such a long journey coupled with the disappointment of a paper-

The Freeborn Slaves.

ended transformation, he was as weak as a bitten frog when he got home and for the next few days, slept like a log of wood.

When KE knocked on his door that early morning, he checked his time and concluded that he was dreaming. Otherwise, "How could any madman dare disturb my sleep this ungodly hour?" he had queried. "…even if the whole palace is on fire!" he fumed.

He wanted to go back to his sleep but bang! bang! bang! on his door brought him back to reality.

"Okwute? Okwute?" he called, thinking it was his housemaid, "You have gone mad beyond cure to bang on my…" but,

Bang! Bang! Bang! Bang! Came the knock even louder threatening to pull down the whole building.

"Open it!" came a hoarse voice that made him shrink immediately making everything in him go under cover.

As he nervously fumbled and tumbled, it became almost impossible for him to unlock his door.

"Your time remains ten seconds o," sounded the voice again in some kind of pidgin and… ***gwaragada!*** came the door crashing on top of Ezenobi even before he could explain that he was opening the door.

The Freeborn Slaves.

Now, before Ezenobi, stood many men and another thing that looked like a human being. He couldn't count how many of them there were because of the darkness and the rain. But behind them, he saw Okwute his maid standing like a zombie and apparently unconscious. In a split second, Ezenobi noticed that they had no gun but he wasn't sure.

As he tried to properly wake up from sleep, his sleepy mind deceived him that he could take on two of them at a time without stress. At least to kill one of them before they killed him. He was not able to recognize any one of the assailants except for Okwute whom he saw at a moment when torchlight flashed.

"Even an about-to-be-executed person has to try and run for his life," he encouraged himself.

For an instant, his mind told him to go slap two out of them at a time to show them what it meant to wake a prince from his sleep. He made to obey his instincts but "Ahhh!" he shouted, he had been transfixed.

"We are not going to hurt you Eze if you co-operate with us though of course you must," said KE the Killer Eternal. To Ezenobi's surprise, the hoarse voice was from the tiny thing among them.

"Who are you?" he questioned helplessly, "and what do you want?"

The Freeborn Slaves.

"Hmmn? Is it necessary?" KE asked in mock laughter, "But if you must know, we used to be kidnappers but today we are 'man-nappers' because you are already a man".

On hearing KE say that he made to go slap him to prove to him and all of them that they were not mates and that it had been their worst choice to barge in on him uninvited. He made to move again and rush KE in obedience to the anger that had built up in him but alas, his legs were still rooted at his spot.

"There's no point trying," KE told him, "otherwise I would have blown off your puffed dollop head."

"Shu... shut ...up!" Eze stammered angrily even as he became terrified at the sight of the short gun KE brandished. Just then, he noticed among them a man who was in a particular position. He also saw another man who was equally unconscious like Okwute.

"We are here to take you, young man!" KE informed Ezenobi.

"You are the biggest foolish joker!" Ezenobi fired back.

"Take whatever personal effect you may need because the road would be too far," BigChild put in calmly.

The Freeborn Slaves.

"Follow you to where?" the prince asked, really frightened and trembling now. He was taken by such a storm that his confusion and helplessness cannot be described.

"Okwuteee!" Ezenobi called his maid, "Why did you allow these men in here? In fact, where is everybody? Eh!" he started shouting. "Nobody has heard me? Eh! Oh, what is happening here?" Those questions were mere rhetoric.

Against his will and without anybody pushing him, Prince Ezenobi found himself following the strangers. When they passed by the sitting room, he saw the entire royal household including His Royal Highness, the king, Igwe Anunti sleeping soundly on the bare floor. They had all been gathered to the Obi in a sleepwalking fashion and allowed to wake up whenever the hypnotist's power left them. Only then did he realize what had hit them.

The Freeborn Slaves.

Chapter 36.

"Hey, stop there!" ordered Akparata the chief vigilante who has arrived with his men, "what do you think you are doing... taking our prince away? Oh no! Not just now..."

There had been total darkness except for the torchlight KE had. The men of the vigilante relied on their knowledge of the terrain to move around in the night. Abo tried his charm but it was of no effect. He chanted and chanted but the vigilante men were unshaken. KE and BigChild who relied on the assurance of Abo's presence were found hiding behind him. As the potency of Abo and his charms has become questionable, fear gripped them all. The men of the vigilante on realizing their victory advanced forward but foolish as it sounds, the kidnappers tried to run. They were caught and given the beating of their life. But that was just the beginning of their tales as the men of the vigilante soon began to bind them up for onward submission to the king.

"Ah! Ah! Ah!" came from different men of the vigilante. Their arms and muscles were a kind of suddenly cramping up. As they looked, they saw the young oldie among their assailants having a field day laughing at them. They were confused and wondered whether he had anything to do with their pains. Then, as they noticed they had succeeded, Abo tried one last time and surprisingly, he disappeared with BigChild leaving KE and the third person behind. The men of the vigilante searched and searched but

The Freeborn Slaves.

only found KE who had fallen into a ditch and may have broken his spinal cord. No attention was given to him as they said it was better he is left to die shortly after. The third person who had equally abruptly regained consciousness took to his heels too. They saw him but couldn't care less. They know his Osu parents well enough and would deal with all of them later. Their concern was to ensure that their prince was in order and safe.

Surprisingly, Abo and BigChild found themselves at the Ochete shrine. There was nobody in the shrine except for the stinking chilling cold, numerous ribbons and down-turned earthen pots. To further compound the surprise, BigChild found the third person right in the shrine already asleep. With mouths agape, he wondered how bizarre things can get sometimes. He and Abo fell asleep or so BigChild thought. When morning came, Ochete's chief priest came, and even though he too was surprised, he didn't know why he had to hide and feed BigChild. Although he had melted right inside himself, BigChild didn't know whether Abo was as surprised. When he came to, he couldn't find his compatriots Abo or the third person, and yet the kindness from a total stranger inside a stinking shrine was really unbelievable. He couldn't figure out where he was yet the stranger continued to tell him that all was well. But then his horror refused to abate each time he looked at the Ochete's blood-stained altar to behold the numerous masquerade heads dripping fresh red-hot blood unto a ribbon-tied calabash. Was it his mind playing tricks on him or something, he didn't know but

The Freeborn Slaves.

something kept telling him that the blood was that of human beings. And just when he thought the man was becoming more than too friendly, he came in with a machete which he promptly lowered his bulk and began to sharpen.

"Where are my friends?" BigChild asked fearfully, "The people I was with?"

The priest simply glanced at him and looked away.

"Please… where are my... my... my... friends?" BigChild stammered,

"Which friends?" the priest retorted harshly, "go and find them with your dead parents!" he finished as he cast BigChild yet another wicked glance that sent the big boy's spirit racing out of him. BigChild opened his mouth to say something but was too scared to say a thing.

"You wander into my shrine and still have the effrontery to ask me where's your friends… did I invite you?" Ochukor the priest went on as he looked up from filing his machete, "I'm only the handmaid of the gods and I'm only doing with you what they said I should."

Bigchild tried to stand and run but was too weak to lift a finger. Was it the sleep that sapped all his energy or did the foods he ate without questions contain something else? He thought of how paradoxical life could be and wondered how a friendly face suddenly turned to this wicked grin.

The Freeborn Slaves.

Chapter 37.

That same day, Igwe the king, and his council wasted no time before throwing a bash for the vigilante to thank and congratulate them for their gallantry and victory in repelling the enemy. Every member of the Owere village was invited to the impromptu Ofalla and they all ate and drank to their satisfaction even though some didn't know the reason for the bash. It would be taboo for the villagers to know that the Igwe could be harmed with charms or that the palace was overrun by strangers and the prince was almost taken away. They all ate and drank that so many forgot their children and many more including the vigilante did not know how the night turned to day.

As a mark of honor for the vigilante and the village gods who guided them, the house of Ajuwa, the boy who was believed to have come with the kidnappers, was razed down. He denied it but the Owere vigilante didn't need the ascent of an Osu before they dealt with him. They reported how they knew he was the traitor who brought the invaders that intended to kidnap Ezenobi the prince. It was divine intervention that saved the entire household from being annihilated.

When the Ochete priest released his victim deep in the night, BigChild was more than confused. He came out alone but when he rubbed his eyes to see clearly where he was, he saw Abo and the third person right by his side. He didn't know what question to ask but hoped to ask them sometime later.

The Freeborn Slaves.

"Come with me," Abo urged him and he promptly followed him. The palace was like an unguarded no-man's land when they got there and this time around, Abo only had to use his juju powers on them just to be double sure.

For the second time, Ezenobi found himself in a Deja Vu. Against his will and without anybody pushing him, he yet again found himself following the strangers. As they passed by the sitting room again, he saw yet again the entire royal household sleeping on the bare floor. Then did he truly realize that indeed there was a snake in the raffia.

The Freeborn Slaves.

Chapter 38.

Deep into the morning after several hours of unconsciousness, Ukwueze, Igwe Anunti's second wife woke up with a start.

"*Ezechitoke Abiama*! God" she began. "Again? where am I sleeping?" "Ho! Ho! Ho!" "*Bia*, what is happening here? Who is doing this and bringing us all into this place?" "Okwute! Dimgba!" She called their guards, maids, maidens, and palace servants one after the other. "Come, they are all here." She was surprised. She stood up, touched her husband, and called his name but all she got in response was the sound of Igwe Anunti's snoring nose and mouth.

Igwe Anunti, palace guards, wives, princes, and princesses were all sound asleep on the bare floor. Igwe Anunti knew herbs, but Abo's hands are more acceptable to the gods. As they say, what a man can, another man can "uncan" it. Every man has one head, but some heads are actually bigger than others. The hypnotist's power proved that. His victims, the royal household were like sleep-starved people who weren't even ready to wake up any time soon. They simply slept away their life.

As none of them responded to her calls, Ukwueze started wailing and soon the whole palace was flooded by the villagers who came to know why. They were all amazed how such a thing could happen to an entire household without any

The Freeborn Slaves.

of them defying it. They had never seen or heard of something like that before. "It's terrible!" they all agreed.

This time, practically no one cared about the security implication of exposing that the palace was overrun. Some men who were around carried Igwe Anunti to his bedroom and allowed him to sleep on. The previous experience showed them that the victims would wake up when the effect left them. All he did was fart, heave a sigh of relief and continue snoring.

It was Chukwude who asked Ukwueze what actually happened. Just then she remembered that there was a time she came out to urinate the other night of the attack and saw some men who were in their compound. She remembered seeing Okwute and Achuzie following just like zombies behind them. She said that one of the men had his hands in the air while he muttered some strange words and when she wanted to speak out and ask who they were she couldn't. She had lost her vocal cords. Was it Achuzie or Ajuwa they wondered.

Chukwude and others present shuddered as he inferred that maybe they had punished the Ajuwa family wrongly. Nobody had ever heard of something like that. This time, after waiting for long and the king and other family members were not forth-coming, they all agreed to call the village Dibia- the Agu Ngwu, who followed them without delay. On arrival, he emptied his "*Akpakoro*" bag on the floor. He was so baffled that he didn't know where to begin but anyhow,

The Freeborn Slaves.

there must be a way to crack this nut. There would always be a way to carry the man with waist pain for the journey to be made.

Firstly, he brought out the ***Ekwe*** (wooden gong), bit on it as he said under his breath- ***"Anyi kme eka, anyi teme egwu"*** implying that they would knock on the door of the spirits and dance, whilst bringing out the '***Afa***", divination beads. He laid them on the ground and began his invocations and incantations in some strange '***Afa***' language;

He threw debris of the kola nuts as he called on the market days to come and eat the kola nuts. After this, he danced and danced, then brought out the eagle's feathers, held them in both hands and walked around Igwe Anunti. He chanted incantations and then explained that the eagle is a rare bird and so is the solution to the rare situation at hand.

"Ehh," he replied to the '***Afa***' which had supposedly spoken silently to him, "My spiritual eagle shall fly to the far and wide, to the hills and valleys and from the rising of the sun to its setting to find the solution to our problem," he had explained. Then he brought out the small calabash where he kept the sun-dried concoction including the intestines of little creatures and brought out what he called the intestine of an ant. He explained that as little as the ant is, so will it be able to trace the smallest details of the strange omen that had befallen Owere village.

He then commanded his spiritual ant to go to work while he put the intestine into the ***'Uruu'*** concoctions he was

The Freeborn Slaves.

preparing and chanted incantations unto the mixture. When the mixture was ready, he carried it in his left hand, red ribbon round his head and held a pussy-cat tail in the right and began to dance round frantically as if in a trance. As he danced, he poured libations on the ground telling it to counter whatever charm was responsible for this omen.

"This is the spiritual eye," he explained of the pussycat tail. "And it shall find the king's spirit wherever he is and reveal it to my eyes," he said referring to his eyes that are closed. After dancing some more for what seemed like an eternity, he was already sweating profusely when he felt he got the message he sought.

"It's Lui Okwuruoha's family," he announced in a hysterical and wild voice that almost awoke Igwe Anunti from his coma.

"But the family was eliminated without a remainder," Chukwude tried to remind him.

"That's true," supported another man half-heartedly.

"How come the link?" they all wondered halfheartedly too. They feared to incur the priest's wrath or that of the gods.

"Are you sure you saw people enter this palace?" Chukwude asked directing his gaze towards Ukwueze, "Or was it spirits you saw?"

The Freeborn Slaves.

"I am sure I saw them and truly nothing had happened to me then," she affirmed.

"Do you doubt the potency of Ngwu's powers?" Agu Ngwu sharply asked directing his gaze to Chukwude, "Or are you in any way trying to suggest that I may be lying?"

"Not in any way, **nna anyi Agu**," Chukwude defended himself, "It's just that I…"

"Better watch your tongue, young man!" Agu Ngwu snapped, "Or Ngwu would just prove to you now now that he has powers."

"As a matter of fact," the priest went on, "I see them running away with somebody from this palace," Agu stated. Just then they all noticed for the first time that Ezenobi was not among those sleeping in the Obi.

"Has he come back?" some of the people asked.

"Yes, some nights ago," confirmed Ukwueze amidst sobs.

"Don't mind him!" snapped another, "ask him why he drank himself to stupor yesterday."

"When he was molding the big fufu in order to eat more than everyone else, he didn't claim not to know it was to welcome the prince"

The Freeborn Slaves.

They went to his room and met his doors ajar but nobody inside.

Ukwueze ran back to wake Ocheze, the first wife, who is also Ezenobi's mother. "***Ogbo m***?" she called, "They have taken away your breast from you o, please wake up," she finished half audibly.

Ocheze continued in her slumber and Ukwueze fainted.

Agu Ngwu, looked at Chukwude with 'you-doubter' kind of look on his face. There was great pandemonium and wailing everywhere. Some women fetched water and poured on Ukwueze, and combined with Agu's incantations, they resuscitated her.

Meanwhile, Igwe the king had woken from his juju-induced astral travel. He wondered why there was wailing and chaos all over his palace.

"Was I dead?" he asked himself. "What kind of sleep did I fall into not to know when all these legs entered my palace? For how long have I slept?" He continued pouring questions at no one in particular without anyone to answer them. The wailing continued as people continued to call Ocheze his wife.

Those at his bedside had all rushed out to know why people were shouting and wailing and calling Ocheze and Ukwuee, and so were not there when Igwe woke up. They thought that maybe someone had died.

The Freeborn Slaves.

As the fog in his mind began to clear, Igwe Anunti tried to stand from his bed but was too weak to lift a finger.

"Ah!" he said in a distressed voice, "Am I sick or my wife dead?" he wondered.

"Somebody tell me," he tried calling out but alas, his voice was on leave too. After several attempts to rise from his bed or call out to the people outside failed, he let himself be.

Just then Ichie Nnanna entered and shouted that the king was awake. This calmed Igwe Anunti down a bit. Before now, he had concluded that he was dead and buried and already in the land of the spirits with his ancestors whom he believed were the voices outside deciding his case.

People rushed in and found him being helped up by two of his aides. It was as if the royal household was given a sedative, each with the right dose that would last for a given length of time.

As Igwe was being helped up, Okwute woke up followed by Okpoko. Okwute returned to normalcy immediately. Soon he began to spill the beans of how this and that happened. He explained how after the bash, all of them, the guards fell asleep all at once. On his own, he was half asleep. He heard the elderly one as he spoke before he grabbed his hand. "I wanted to fight him but my hands froze in the air," he said. He explained that the man muted out something upon him

The Freeborn Slaves.

and all he could do was follow them like a zombie. "And I showed him where everyone slept," he said sheepishly.

"Did you recognize anyone among them?" Chukwude asked.

"Yes, I saw Achuzie on the two occasions but it seemed he was also unconscious of what he was doing."

"So it was Achuzie? But why did they say Ajuwa…" asked Ichie Nnanna. "This whole thing is becoming complicated every passing moment; why would they take Achuzie?" he further queried.

When the king had recovered a little bit, Agu Ngwu took him in confidence and explained to him what they had been discussing.

"But Eze told me…" the king was saying, "that every one of Lui's household was… was…, burnt alive," he tearfully finished more to himself.

"Are you doubting me or the gods?" the priest challenged.

"Nooo, wise one," Igwe Anunti defended himself to avoid the wrath of Ngwu deity, "You never told me lies before. So… what, what shall we do now, but come, where is Ezenobi?" he suddenly remembered. Agu Ngwu kept quiet and was not willing to look him in the eyes.

The Freeborn Slaves.

"Eze! The king called, "Ezenobi... My prince! Ezeeeeeee! Where is my prince? So they still succeeded? Where is my heir?" Igwe forgot his manners and was calling his dear son hoping to hear him answer. "What happened to him? Somebody say something to me now, where is my son, Ezenobi? Tell me if he is dead, Agu, the truthful one and I promise to be myself," Igwe Anunti vowed even as he wept.

"Igweee," Agu Ngwu began, "They took Ezenobi your..."

Before Agu Ngwu could finish what he had to say, Igwe Anunti was already having a meeting with maybe the spirits. They tried to revive him from that morning till evening all to no avail. Long into the evening, Agu begged to be allowed to go see his family and was obliged. On his way home, he shuddered at the many revelations he had been given while he was pouring out the libation.

In one of the revelations, he saw the crown being taken off Igwe Anunti's head in a very strange manner. As he and his family members, and the entire Owere villagers struggled to grab the crown back from the mighty strange hand that de-crowned him, the crown was taken and placed on a head that seemed to be a nobody. He couldn't make out the face that owned the head.

In another, he saw himself fall asleep and when he awoke, Owere villagers were jubilating that their kidnapped king had returned.

The Freeborn Slaves.

"But the crown eluded all Owere people, how come they were rejoicing that their kidnapped king had come back?" he wondered, "But everyone there was happy" at least that one he was sure of.

He smelt some ratty troubles around the corner but he was warned not to tell anyone about this vision for now.

"Maybe, Igwe the king would not make it out of this coma, and Ezenobi would return from the land of the kidnappers and become the Igwe. Yes! That's it," he concluded.

The Freeborn Slaves.

Chapter 39.

Igwe Anunti woke up with a start, nearly at dawn the next day. He pitied his palace for what it had become in so short a time. He already had troubles enough to last him three lifetimes. This one vengeance he took has refused to go away. Apart from the many sleepless nights he had had since that black night of revenge, something kept reporting to his ears that he had bitten more than he could chew. He was no longer fighting mere mortals alone.

"But I am the custodian of the tradition," he assured himself, "and as such, I am supposed to protect it. I only killed some Osu who killed members of a royal household. It has always been our culture to avenge the death of any freeborn and that's exactly what I did," he exonerated himself. "So, I'm right."

He has been hit beyond what he ever expected. Two of his daughters had died in their husband's homes three nights after the revenge. A mysterious fire just broke out in their respective homes and their lives went with it. The mystery there was that the fire only killed them and burnt things that belonged to them.

His second son Ohuabunwa had sent his wife packing seven days after the vengeance night. When questioned why he sent his wife packing, he simply said he was tired of married life. To crown it, Ohuabunwa had refused to go to his revenue office at the Orie market.

The Freeborn Slaves.

Igwe Anunti didn't have many children, but the ones he had, he made sure they had all they wanted. *Ezechitoke* God simply chose to punish him in his children. His hopes had been on Ezenobi whom he had sent abroad to study. His only problem with Ezenobi was his choice of wife- a white lady.

"*Ezechitoke,* don't forsake me o, please," he prayed to his God, "I am fighting a just course. Our people say that a wise child kills that which killed his father so that what killed his father would not kill him, and I owe that to my father," he agreed, "So where have I gone wrong?"

He questioned his *chi* and tears rolled down his cheek. He called on all the gods and deities in the village and beyond to join and fight his fight. He begged them to help him find his heir. His sorrow went on for days, weeks, and months yet his heir was still missing. He refused to be admonished that crying was not good for his age and position.

As misery after misery continued to visit the royal family, friends diminished in number and even cabinet meetings became scanty; no longer frequent as usual. The king has not found his feet, let alone have time for women and palm wine as usual, and as such, many sycophants relocated or took their praise singing and gossip to some other places.

"The lion's legs are wounded and even squirrels have come for their debts." Igwe Anunti reflected, "The mighty Iroko tree has fallen and the birds have all taken flight. What a life! Yes, the palm tree had fallen and even women now climb it."

The Freeborn Slaves.

Chapter 40.

When the fog started clearing from his eyes and the smoke from his brain, Ezenobi woke up in a strange room that had nothing in it except for a very high-up-the-wall window and the entrance door which he was sure was securely locked. The dark light that showed was from behind a hurriedly fixed ceiling fan from a very high deck probably upstairs. In the semi-darkness, he could make out that the place was a large warehouse.

He didn't know whether it was day or night how long he had been there or how long since he slept, but surely he knew that it must have been very long.

Just then he heard,

"Yes, he is awake now…" a voice said, "Are the papers ready… no problems men, you can always trust me."

....

"Ezenobi is alive but nowhere near Owere village," was all they heard from every "*Dibia*" they consulted within and outside Owere. On what his future held, they all said, "It was not yet clear."

By the middle of the seventh month after the kidnap, Igwe Anunti, just like his palace, was already a shadow of his former self. The village was not left out. It had turned into a ghost village filled with living dead. Igwe's health had so

The Freeborn Slaves.

deteriorated that people wondered what he was still doing staying alive. He already had a partial stroke that impaired the right-hand side of his body. The stroke had refused to respond to any medication, local or foreign. Moreover, it was a serious tug-of-war to open his mouth to feed him his food or drugs as he had become suicidal. He had so wished for death that even death was scared to come anywhere near him. He could even kill death itself out of the joy and passion with which he sought it. People had so anticipated his death that when he finally died on the nineteenth of December, it was no longer news. The only problem for some concerned villagers was the absence of an heir to continue the dynasty.

....

Now, since Ezenobi had disappeared, and Ohuabunwa was three-quarters a lunatic. It therefore meant that after a one-year period of mourning, the kingdom's crown would be moved to their nearest kinsman Okafor.

Okafor was an upright man who believed in God. The mere thought of him becoming the next king frightened many of the palace chiefs who were birds of a feather with Igwe Anunti. He would surely open up their bellies and reveal all the bad things they had eaten. He professed a new creed and religion which was against greed and corruption. He had shown signs that he was against the tradition of corruption in the village thus they saw him as a saboteur or even a traitor.

....

The Freeborn Slaves.

Pa Lui, The Don, made money irrespective of how he made it, and he had connections too. He knew that his wealth was ill-gotten thus he tried to use it to fill the ill of his society. They had consulted him through a medium that Abo claimed represented the giant *Akpu* tree of their village and to BigChild's surprise, he heard his father's voice though shrill but loud and clear enough as he shrieked out directives on who and who to meet and what steps to take.

Abo and BigChild opened the package from the registry and marveled at what they discovered. The precision with which The Don wrote down everything that had happened was amazing.

The story and the will were both written by experts in a very concise manner. The story contains every vital detail of The Don's family genealogy, the reason for the story, and the possible solution to the predicament of his people. Following the story, even a man thrown down from the moon could trace Ogbodu village- their home.

He had planned to use the Owere people and especially the royal family's follies to teach all and sundry a memorable bitter lesson. When the idea came into his mind, it was almost late but he encouraged himself and sent Achuzie to the best school outside their village. Even though Don Lui deviated, Achuzie was through secondary school when The Don disappeared.

When the two of Achuzie and Ezenobi were born, the village was agog with the news of yet another separated twin. It was

The Freeborn Slaves.

so rife in the two villages that even the king had to send for Achuzie's mother just to behold the unwanted son. He confirmed the news and the resemblance but added that the boy was a rejected seed.

"Like father like son; Like minds work together," BigChild confirmed.

The Freeborn Slaves.

Chapter 41.

Just when the businesses were booming and the staff and customers were all taking a liking to the BigChild's management style, he was closing shops especially the loud and notorious businesses that brought attention to him. Before they knew what to say again, they heard he had given a percentage of the proceeds to the poor. Before handing over the businesses to the new owners, he settled some selected workers whose businesses were sold including the Booty-for-all girls especially Ijeuwa whom he believed prompted him to action. Though he did not reveal his mission to Ijeuwa, he enjoined her to pray for him and to ensure she obtained an education. He only told her he had a need to go under but promised to take her back to Ogbodu village when he was done with his mission. Finally, many of The Don's known businesses were closed down and sold off, and furthermore, BigChild was nowhere to be found.

While the villagers battled with the health and eventual death of their king, Abo, Ezenobi, BigChild, and Achuzie were at Dr Hamsil's hospital. Dr Hamsil was a friend of The Don's when he was in Nigeria. He worked at The Dynamic Hospital (T.D.H), Lekki before leaving for further studies. He loved Don Lui's charisma and guts. There in the overseas, he was working in a general hospital, and had a private hospital.

BigChild had people who helped him smuggle the unconscious parties through the porous borders. They got the

The Freeborn Slaves.

visas however they could and are now in the hospital with the doctor they liked.

Now abroad, BigChild engaged the services of the best experts in all facets of their plan. The team comprised of plastic surgeons, phoneticians, attitude trainers, and all behavioral training specialists. Don't you forget, the best hypnotist was equally around and together they made a perfect team.

They all had a singular goal of transferring, transforming, and whatever trans… you can manufacture provided it would help to make Achuzie become Ezenobi.

While some worked on the physical attributes of Achuzie, others worked on his psychic, spiritual, mental, behavioral, and all other attributes.

Since Achuzie and Ezenobi were a kind of sentimentally-separated twins, it shouldn't be too difficult for the team. The scars and cuts on Achuzie who was just a village hunter before The Don's intervention won't be much problem to handle. The people that had the greatest problem were the phoneticians. Though Ezenobi speaks in the native tongue of the Owere people, the intonation has been affected by the American environment. Achuzie had lived all his life in the village and attended school at an old age when his tongue had become shaped just for the Ogbodu dialect. Whatever the case, their mandate was to make Achuzie begin to look, smile, smell, think, talk, walk, and in fact do everything

The Freeborn Slaves.

exactly like Ezenobi. He must be Ezenobi in all ramifications- period.

Even when this idea was sold to him by his friend, The Don never took Talamorr seriously for telling him such a thing.

"How can you tell me that?" he had questioned, "to change people's natural look, are you God?"

"The Don, you have made the money," Talamorr had said, "and that's part of what money can do. "

Even when The Don saw it in the entertainment channels on the TV, he dismissed it with a wave of hands calling it a movie acted by some experts.

"Some men change themselves to women these days," Talamorr had said emphatically.

"Yes I know," replied The Don comically, "some humans changed to gods too, and I've seen them."

It was Dr. Hamsil that convinced him of the possibility of all that and even told him he could do it himself.

Three weeks into the transformation agenda, all hopes were almost lost on Achuzie's cooperation. They had reasoned that it would be better to infuse the academics into Achuzie before other pieces of training. Though he had had education, it was not to be compared to that of Ezenobi so they said that that would put him in the right mindset and reasoning ability for other trainings. But somewhere in the

The Freeborn Slaves.

middle of the process and under the intense power of the hypnotist, even Abo and some team members were ready to quit. They were convinced that no further progress could be made with Achuzie.

Under hypnosis, Ezenobi would be talking like a canary about his family, his origin, his life, in fact, everything they wanted to know about him. He talked about his escapades and how he planned to live in the future. The most important information was the revelation about how they planned and carried out the operations on the night the Lui family returned. He mentioned the names of all the people involved. That was fantastic but then came to Achuzie. Any attempt to ask him about his life and his brain would go blank. He would just sit straight with his mouth shut tightly.

When Abo felt that Achuzie's case was becoming impossible for him in spite of his spiritual and mystical prowess, they invited some Arabian and Indian hypnotists and masters of esoteric powers of spiritism to help elicit information from him. With all their combined efforts, success remained a mirage. His case was so bad because he would not give out information and he would not receive either.

They would work on him dusk to dawn, dawn to dusk but afterward, he would not remember a single thing he was told. The situation so infuriated them all that they agreed he was being remotely controlled from the village. Even BigChild nearly gave up but he just stubbornly refused to be frustrated.

The Freeborn Slaves.

He promised to increase their fees provided they exercised some more patience. It was two weeks later that Dr. Summila, a friend of Hamsil's who worked in the hospital with him came and suggested they seek Achuzie's consent in the whole thing. They tried it and it worked wonders. Just to be reminded of the circumstances surrounding his birth was enough to trigger the adrenalin in him to the boiling point.

With the secret revealed to him, Achuzie vowed never to be any impediment to the success of the landmark dream. True to his vow, he gave his consent and never gave any trouble again. He confessed that while in school on a certain sunny day and while still wide awake, he had a daytime dream where a strange voice spoke to him from the midst of an inexplicable atmospheric effervescence. The voice had spoken to him about the freedom struggle a few days before the kidnap. He couldn't understand it and thus didn't know how to tell anyone about it. He was still brooding over the whole thing when the voice advised him to go home and he obeyed only for him to get home and be kidnapped.

They had just begun to enjoy their work on Achuzie when suddenly Ezenobi defied the Abo's hypnosis and woke up, eyes shining like torchlight, and he started shouting, "Where is Cassandra?"

They were all puzzled: Cassandra was the staff nurse who brought something for Dr. Hamsil. While leaving, her body brushed against Ezenobi. That singular body contact fetched

The Freeborn Slaves.

Ezenobi's spirit from the world of the living dead of hypnosis and set it racing back to abrupt consciousness. Unfortunately for him, when his spirit finally made it to the physical world, Cassandra had left.

Every effort to work on Ezenobi either to teach how he placed his tongue when pronouncing certain words never worked again. He kept demanding to see Cassandra.

They all became afraid to bring in Cassandra because they didn't know what transpired in the spiritual realm that abruptly awoke him to demand for her. They considered Cassandra an agent sent by the devil himself who was sent to disrupt their work. They waited for whatever was responsible for it to subside all to no avail thus they decided to consult with Cassandra.

....

Dr. Hamsil and the wonderful twosome of Abo and BigChild were seated over some wine in The Daula Café, the best restaurant around, over some drinks and a bottle of water before Abo who always never opened or drank any.

Inside their special ward, Achuzie was under serious hypnotic powers while Ezenobi was in chains for his refusal to be hypnotized. They didn't want to sedate him. They locked the main door behind them and set out to meet Cassandra. Dr. Hamsil was actually enjoying himself in all the episodes.

The Freeborn Slaves.

Cassandra was more than surprised when Dr. Hamsil invited her for lunch. It had never happened before and now when it did, it is at the most expensive café around- The Daula Café. If Dr. Hamsil was not already married to his wives, she would have thought it to be in connection with marriage.

"Or is he going to ask me to be his mistress?" she wondered. "But he had never looked at me with any special interest."

Cassandra knew that she was a beautiful girl. "Is he going to introduce me to someone else?" questions upon questions, yet no answers to any. She would have asked him to explain but Dr. Hamsil was a responsible man before her and besides, he was her boss.

"It can only be something good that would make him bring me to this kind of place," she encouraged herself.

She was disappointed or rather upset when she came and met a team of three men. Her hopes sank because even though she was single, none of the two of Abo and BigChild appealed to her fancy and besides, they never showed her any green light since their stay in the private ward.

"Hello Cassandra," greeted Dr. Hamsil, "please sit down."

"Thank you, Doc," Cassandra replied, her heart pounding and threatening to break the rib cage.

The Freeborn Slaves.

"You are most welcome Cassandra," BigChild put in.

"Thank you," she answered as she guessed over and over what the meeting would be all about. However, she was reassured by the friendly faces looking at her. She could also sense the fear in their eyes too. She could almost hear their hearts pounding beneath their chests. Somehow she was beginning to suspect they had come to ask her for a favor. She couldn't make out what it was but she could feel the desperation in their eyes.

A more-than-necessary moment elapsed before anybody spoke again. Dr. Hamsil purposely allowed that to enable everyone especially Cassandra time to acclimatize.

"You know these people now," Dr Hamsil said to Cassandra just casually while they waited for the waiter to bring their demand.

"Yes," she slightly nodded.

"This is BigChild and..."

"And I would like to know about the big dad and the big mum," Cassandra teased wondering at such a name. "What a funny name," she concluded.

"We equally have the BigGirl o," BigChild said trying very hard to put up a good appearance even as the BigGirl's memory haunted him inwardly.

The Freeborn Slaves.

"Ehhh?" she marveled.

"And what about the big Daddy and the big Mummy?" she joked.

"They are all there," BigChild lied again.

"And this is Abo," Dr. Hansil went on, "And, men, this is Cassandra, of course, you both know her," finished Dr. Hamsil.

This "of course, you both know her" sounded somehow to her. She equally knew them but he didn't use such expression but formally introduced them to her.

Just then the waiter brought what they had ordered.

"It may surprise you that I have to begin this conversation, Cassandra," BigChild began, "But it is for a reason."

Dr. Hamsil nodded in agreement urging him to go on.

Cassandra concluded she was right in her guess; they needed her help.

"As they say," BigChild continued, "one who is fed is the one to bring mouth closer, and the goat always follows who had the fodder."

Cassandra simply looked on and nodded where she agreed.

Tony Ik Odoh

The Freeborn Slaves.

"We have been here for months like you know, but the success of our stay is being jeopardized by a serious problem at the moment," BigChild stated.

"Does it have anything to do with me?" she questioned apprehensively.

"Yes," answered Abo and BigChild simultaneously, "You are the solution," BigChild stated.

"You are an African," BigChild went on, "Though a citizen here and you have lived here all these years."

Cassandra just looked on wondering what he was up to.

"I believe you won't decline to help a fellow African if need be especially…"

This annoyed Cassandra almost to the point of no return.

"What's the meaning of that? What's the matter with you? Are you trying to blackmail me?" she fumed.

"Calm down, please, Cassandra," Dr. Hamsil pleaded.

"What has my being an African got to do with whatever your problem is? I help whoever I choose to help."

"I'm sorry," BigChild pleaded.

"I'm sorry, please," BigChild said again. His ego had been wounded seriously.

The Freeborn Slaves.

"Just say whatever you have to say and let me out of here," she continued fuming.

Though BigChild was wrong in his choice of words, he never expected it to make the girl flare up like that. "Times change," BigChild thought. If not because he was begging her for something that he needed at all costs, he would have taught "this little brat how to talk to a Capone" he thought to himself, "But then, there must be something to remove from a meat in order to eat it" he agreed. After all, he decided to go under just to accomplish this mission.

"It was a wrong choice of words, he never meant to blackmail you," Dr. Hamsil pacified her. "It's about what they have come here to do," Dr. Hamsil took over the talking. "He was only being nervous, and as it is, you are free to cooperate with us or not."

"What is it about?" she asked.

"You know his brother in the private ward?" said the doctor.

"Yes, what about him?" she asked.

"The one whose face is covered?" said the doctor.

"Yes," she replied.

"Something happened on Tuesday after you brought my kits." He looked at her face for any clue to anything but her face was expressionless.

The Freeborn Slaves.

"As soon as you left, he regained consciousness and started demanding to see Cassandra."

"Cassandra?" she queried, "Maybe his girlfriend's name is Cassandra."

"No!" Hamsil cut in, "Even the men here said they never heard any name that sounded like Cassandra, and the guy in question lived in America."

"Then he may be calling his girlfriend or are you suspecting he may be referring to me?" she wondered.

"Yes, there's no doubt about that, he refers to you," affirmed the Doc. "In fact, he has refused to be worked on since then but kept asking to see you."

"Then why have you not called me since?" she questioned.

"We didn't know what happened, whether you knew him before or something," "We don't know whether he had come here before or you've been to America."

"No," she said, "How would I know him when I have not even seen his face since he came here?"

As she just said that, she recalled how the man's body quivered when her body touched his. She had felt some sensation run through her but she too didn't know how to explain that. She had hoped to unravel the mystery when next she entered the ward but the opportunity never came as

The Freeborn Slaves.

she was promptly transferred to another ward away from Dr. Hamsil and his patients

The Freeborn Slaves.

Chapter 42.

Before now, Cassandra had been plagued in her dreams by a man whose face was covered by a veil. Each time she slept, she saw a man who followed her about telling her to "do whatever they ask you to do."

"Who are you and who are the "they"?" she always asked the man, but the man would simply reply, "Do whatever they asked you to do."

She had on one occasion tried to unveil the man's face but her hands couldn't finish removing the veil that covered the face. The cloth kept unwinding endlessly until she got exhausted and woke up. Then on a certain night, the man had removed the veil by himself to reveal his face. She could still recall the face and could recognize it anywhere.

On the day of the body contact she recalled, the way the face was covered was exactly like that of the man in her dreams.

She had been so obsessed with this nightmare that it was no longer news to people around her including Dr. Hamsil. Even her personal psychologist once advised her to stop working with psychiatrists and hypnotists. They reasoned it could be her daytime experience that hunted and taunted her in the night.

"We want to ask you," Dr. Hamsil began cutting into her reminiscence, "If you have or know anything that would help us?"

The Freeborn Slaves.

"We would like you to help us, please," said Abo and BigChild in unison.

"Can I see him?" she asked.

"Sure," they said, all at once.

"I mean; can I see his face?"

"In fact, he is wide awake now," BigChild put in, "with no veil over his face."

"What would you want me to do?" she asked.

"Sorry," Hamsil started, "We were going to ask you that because we believe you possess the answer"

"Me?" she asked surprised, "Come, what's the agenda in this whole thing?"

"Not to worry" BigChild cut in, "You shall be told the faintest details of all you need to know," and with that, Cassandra was given the whole story.

"How can you just invite me here and think you can make me part of the freedom struggle in your village?" she asked and stood up to leave but Dr. Hamsil begged her to please help.

"Please nobody meant that," Abo put in, "It's just circumstances that warranted it."

The Freeborn Slaves.

"In fact, we just want you to go and see him," said BigChild, "and let events unfold by themselves."

"Yes," added Dr. Hamsil and Abo.

Cassandra wanted to storm out of the place but only stayed behind because she wanted to unravel the mystery surrounding her own predicament, and not merely because of their pleas or the money they promised to pay her. The solution to her nightmare stood paramount in her mind more than any act of altruism.

"After I have solved my own problem," she had thought, "you can go to hell and find the solution to your own trouble". She sat down as if she was just doing it for them and was breathing heavily.

"Now when are we going?" she asked.

"Tomorrow," Dr. Hamsil said. They all agreed it would be tomorrow.

....

Before Cassandra showed up the next morning, Ezenobi was back in a coma. He fell asleep as soon as they left to meet with Cassandra and he never woke up again until midnight. He remained calm in his sleep save for so many "Cassandra, do what they ask you to do," he muted. This was a new dimension to it. He only used to demand to see Cassandra, now he added: "Do whatever they ask you to do."

The Freeborn Slaves.

The sentence sounded familiar to Dr. Hamsil, but he couldn't place it. The next morning, immediately after Dr. Hamsil saw Cassandra, he recalled her story and that was that. "Little wonder," he thought.

They went to the private ward together. Even the slightest phrase from the sentence could convince Cassandra that she had found her mystery man. As soon as they entered, it was like a scroll that was written and folded away, and which was then being unwound to reveal all that was written in it.

"Cassandra," she heard in that same voice of her nightmare, "do whatever they ask you to do."

She stood there halfway into the room speechless and transfixed.

"Can I have a word with you please?" she pleaded with Dr. Hamsil in a frightened voice.

"Sure," he obliged her.

"Dr Hamsil," she had begun back in the doctor's office, "I think I have found my mystery man."

"I think so too," Hamsil replied, "He just started this dimension of 'Do whatever they ask you to' thing as we came back from seeing you yesterday."

"Really? This is unbelievable," she put in.

"I was wondering who said something like that to me because it sounded so familiar," the Doc said, "But I only recalled it immediately I saw you this morning."

"How could a dream come so true?" she wondered, "I've been hunted in my dream by a man I didn't know from Adam, and right in my real life I'm face to face with him."

"The picture is a complex one," Hamsil said.

"This world is a complex fairytale," she agreed.

"The story is also a complex one," he opined.

"Which story?" she inquired.

"The one they told you yesterday."

"I am a bit confused," she confessed, "Even the money they are promising does not move me."

"You should be confused no doubt," Dr. Hamsil agreed, "But I have a strong conviction that you have a role in the divine assignment."

"You are scaring me the more," she confessed, "and somehow, sometimes I feel like being manipulated"

"By who?" Dr. Hamsil questioned.

"By them." She answered.

The Freeborn Slaves.

"But this has been happening way back before they even thought of coming to this place. I think you are not being manipulated."

"My nerves are failing me" she confessed.

"Just be yourself and go see him," Hamsil encouraged her.

"No," she said, "I would have to tell my mother first."

"See things for yourself and then know exactly what to tell her," he advised.

"No." she disagreed.

"It's ok, just be yourself. Nobody is going to force you," Hamsil encouraged her.

They went back to the ward together to meet BigChild and Abo. The twosome had been wondering what kept them for so long. They searched their faces for clues but only found fear in Cassandra's eyes. The clutched fists and unsteady steps told as much. Anyhow, they believed that maybe Dr. Hamsil had explained the recent development to her.

As they entered the room, Ezenobi was sound asleep with no veils over his face, he still murmured "Do whatever they ask you to do," tirelessly. She could have fainted. It still remained a mystery to her why she didn't faint. She was still thinking of what to do when all of a sudden Ezenobi started

The Freeborn Slaves.

again and again as if remotely controlled. Like the speed of lightning, he had sat up on the bed and yet repeated all he had been saying; this time in a calmer apologetic voice.

"What do you want me to do?" she asked nobody in particular but however expected BigChild to answer. Ezenobi didn't answer it but kept asking her to do what they asked her to do.

"I will discuss with my mum and get back to you," she replied after BigChild explained her role to her. Ezenobi after that time out never gave further trouble and the rest of the process was a smooth ride to finish.

The Freeborn Slaves.

Chapter 43.

Ezenobi in some of his numerous utterances under hypnosis had disclosed his affairs with Nicole, a black American girl, who was his fiancée. They were already engaged but the problem was that Igwe Anunti, his father, didn't approve of the marriage. He had complained that marrying from America would make Ezenobi a lost son. The king wanted his heir to marry from the Owere village. To him, it was only in Owere that Ezenobi could find a true woman, an African queen who knows the ethics and tradition befitting of a wife of an Igwe the king in the making.

"She is like every one of us," Eze had told his father.

"Would she allow you to take a second wife as befitting of a king?" his father cut in.

"I don't need a second wife," Ezenobi stated.

"You see? I am finished!" the king lamented. "This your Whiteman-bred girl wants to ruin our heritage for us but it won't work! It will never come to pass! Our ancestors would never allow you! She would not know or respect our values," the king argued. "She won't respect our elders and she doesn't know the *Umunna* system that we practice here"

Ezenobi had supported his father in the assassination of the Lui family to secure his blessing for his marriage to Nicole. He had spearheaded the operation to prove to his father that he was worthy of the throne and would support all of the

The Freeborn Slaves.

village traditions. He had even boasted to his father that he would kill them with his own hands and bring the man Lui Okwuruoha himself and his son alive to the palace for the Igwe to see.

That was the reason he couldn't tell his father that the three most important people disappeared that night. He had warned members of the evil gang of the consequences of telling anybody even Igwe Anunti his father, that anybody disappeared. He had reserved to himself the exclusive right of reporting how the operation went. However, every member of the gang went home happier than expected since he made sure they all received extra pay for a 'job' well done.

Two days after the vengeance, Nicole died in a ghastly motor accident but Ezenobi only got to know about it some weeks later. There was no telephone network in the village thus he had gone to Enugu city to call or at least send a telegram to her only for him to receive a message waiting for him about the death of Nicole. He had kept it a secret not even knowing why he kept it a secret himself. Unknown to him by divine design and while he had gone to mourn his fiancée', his spirit had traveled across the wilds, oceans and seas, and was in a faraway land appearing to Cassandra in her dreams, begging her to do whatever she's asked to do.

Now he could connect the dots because though he was not happy to lose his wife then, it baffled him that he did not feel as sad as someone who lost his cherished fiancée. He

The Freeborn Slaves.

suspected that it was his father who was behind the whole thing. He believed his father Igwe Anunti cast a spell on him and his fiancée, and secretly he was holding some grudges against his father over that.

....

Now, what the team wanted Cassandra to do was to act the Ezenobi's Nicole. When the deed must have been done, BigChild and Abo would have taken care of Ezenobi, and Cassandra would go with them to the village and remain Nicole to Achuzie who would have become Ezenobi. She would only be in the village for some time before claiming that she would want to visit her people in Lagos or wherever, and her contract would be over.

The money attached to it was mouthwatering plus she would be liberating some people from bondage. These facts made sense as she discussed it with her mother and she accepted to partake in the freedom struggle.

"Do you trust them?" her mum had asked.

"Not quite," she answered.

"I am afraid."

"I am too."

"It is too risky… with ritual killers on the prowl everywhere there." Her mum said

The Freeborn Slaves.

"The bigger the risk, the better the money," she told her mum.

"And they paid you cash before anything even began scares me,"

"You will enjoy it if I die," she said, "But trust me, Mum, nothing will happen to me."

Seeing the determination in her daughter, she equally yielded. She feared for her daughter's life but too, the money was no doubt very enticing.

Chapter 44.

An unrighteous beginning may by divine cause have a righteous end. Dr. Hamsil, Abo, and BigChild had agreed to give Ezenobi overdoses of some sedative drugs to enable him to join his wicked father and forefathers without pain. On getting to Ezenobi's bedside one fateful morning, they found him stone dead like **Ugwu-Obukpa** the everlasting hill. They wanted him dead and would have killed him all the same, but they were shocked beyond words because Ezenobi never appeared to be sick at all. And now what baffled them most was that although Ezenobi was dead, his face showed with a sort of brightness and radiance they couldn't comprehend; he was smiling, and with this, they knew they were set to go home but they had to wait a little longer.

More than two years had gone by since all the drama began. Achuzie had become a perfect Ezenobi and that was that. They had reasoned that the Achuzie-turned-Ezenobi should live and acclimatize with the Oyibo environment so as to have a real-life experience. They all needed it anyway. Ezenobi equally used the period to brush up on his administrative skills.

On getting home, they met the greatest shock of their lives; Igwe Anunti had died. They never anticipated or thought of something like that, thus there was no prearrangement for that.

The Freeborn Slaves.

Achuzie, sorry, Ezenobi was devastated. There he was all alone. The only companion with him was Cassandra-Turned-Nicole who knew just little about the whole thing.

As a son who lost his father, he was supposed to weep and not just cry. But then, how was he supposed to start crying at the death of the same person who had caused him a lifetime of misery? How could he mourn the same person that had made him mourn all his life? How would anyone expect him to cry rather than jubilate at the demise of a terror and the end of an era of torment for his people? All these questions didn't get any answers.

"But I have to put up appearances or else I would blow the whole thing up," he encouraged himself. He had a serious agenda to accomplish, and besides, he didn't want to curry Abo's or BigChild's wrath.

BigChild had remained in Lagos when they came back while Abo remained a mystery. He kept disappearing and reappearing. They had cooked up the story Achuzie-Ezenobi was to tell the villagers on arrival and it involved only him.

He was to tell the villagers that on the night he was kidnapped, somehow along the way, he didn't know where he got the strength, but he had knocked down the young oldie, killed Achuzie the despicable Osu, and the rest took to their heels after he dealt them some heavy blows that got them calling on their dead mothers. He would then tell them how he had taken his moneybag when they asked him to take his personal effect. He had tiptoed out of the arena and ran

The Freeborn Slaves.

as fast as possible right into a foully and smelly frightening shrine. He had hidden behind the age-long dirty multiple-colored ribbons, stiff-scared; thus, he even had to plead with the spirits of the shrine to pardon his wrongs and save him. And how when morning came, he was tempted to come out but was scared again, when almost immediately he had heard the voices of the remaining members of his assailants searching near the shrine. They had come and peered right into the shrine- the only building around but the stench oozing out of the shrine scared the early-morning sensibilities out of them. He would also tell how the assailants had gone away saying that even a man threatened by the devil to be thrown into the bottomless hell of fire could not hide in that godforsaken shrine. How they had even wondered how blood-tasty a god must be to come to such a place to receive offerings and sacrifices. How they had mocked the chief priest for believing that any god could come down to such a place to receive offerings. That they had hurriedly gone out of the place saying they didn't want to be choked to death by the stench. He had then staggered out of the place and through the Iyiocha River had burst out to the expressway from where he found his way to Enugu, back to Lagos, and back to America.

He would then claim that he found out on getting back to America that Nicole was already pregnant for him though she later lost it and as such he couldn't leave her.

All the cock and bull stories were just to make it look as real as possible that he was Ezenobi. He would say he didn't tell

The Freeborn Slaves.

anybody about his whereabouts because he feared that the assailants would come for him just like his father had feared during the black night era when he was hidden at the Omejenta shrine. He planned to tell his father that he had come home with his wife who is an American citizen with whose help those that perpetrated the heinous crimes would be brought to book.

They had all hoped that the fairytales would work wonders on Igwe Anunti and others and thus convince him about the sense in marrying Nicole and even if he still refused, at least they would have proved he was still the Ezenobi who had a white fiancee. Afterward, he would then waste Igwe Anunti the king, and take over the throne all for the good of the village and the villagers- a selfless heartlessness, as they call it.

....

Now, Igwe Anunti was dead before Ezenobi, his fairytales, and his plans could be unfolded, and that really put him off-guard. He was not prepared for all that, but he had come, and he really wished he was prepared to conquer.

Even as they alighted from the taxi that brought them home, his supposed mother Ocheze fainted. Everyone including Ocheze, her family, and indeed the entire villagers of Owere and Ogbodu, believed that Ezenobi was dead. Even some villagers who had seen their taxi at the **Ama** Owere could not believe it. Some even packed handfuls of sand and threw at him. They believed he was a ghost.

The Freeborn Slaves.

Nevertheless, he managed to rush and hold his "mother" and they all helped to revive her. They welcomed him alright but some busy-bodies immediately began their gossip;

"A foolish idiot that people thought was dead was busy marrying **Oyibo** woman," they said. "Now his father is dead because he thought his heir was no more."

"How could you?" an impatient woman had begun not even waiting for him to enter into the house.

"I will explain," he tried to say.

"Ah ah, please let's allow him to land or to at least enter his room," said some other women.

"I can explain," Ezenobi said again

"Yes, explain to your dead father in the grave," fumed the angry woman.

"Eh?" Ezenobi shouted mouth agape.

"How could he run and not look back to remember his family? Children of nowadays, eh?" they all complained.

"Let's wait until he tells his experience." Said some.

"Which experience?" one questioned, "Can't you see how refreshed he looks? He had been enjoying in the white man's country while everybody languished for him here."

The Freeborn Slaves.

"Ah ah, why are you saying all these now?" asked another.

"He has come back because the time to take over the throne has come," put in the first woman.

"You may not be entirely wrong my sister," said another.

They gossiped and argued back and forth. They didn't know that the Ezenobi that stood before them didn't know "his" room. He and Nicole just stood there like statues. Ezenobi was tactically waiting for any of the maids to help him with the luggage and thus direct him to his room, but it was long in coming. He couldn't cry, he didn't go in he just stood there as many thoughts swept through his brain. With the situation on the ground, he forgot all the tricks he had planned to use. His head was just blank. Each time he wanted to call someone's name, his sibling's name would come. He barely managed to control the situation.

Just when he was about to give up waiting, a woman shouted at the maids to do their duties; take their luggage inside, and prepare their bath water for them.

When Ocheze, his mother, was revived, she only stared at him not saying a word. All efforts by Ezenobi to cry didn't yield any fruit. He just couldn't mourn the demise of the source of his misery. That should have been good riddance to bad rubbish. All the people around excused him saying that he was too shocked to cry at the moment.

The Freeborn Slaves.

"He may actually have not known that his father was dead except on getting home," some tried to excuse him.

A few days later, he learned that his real mother had passed away just months after he was kidnapped and that was when he really wailed. It was just divinity that saved him from calling Mgbafor his mother's name as he cried.

He confided in Cassandra, no, "Nicole" that he wanted to go and visit his people, but she advised him otherwise. "It's too early," she had said. The two were out for a job and they couldn't afford to blow it. They planned a job but they had moved on better than anyone could have imagined. Nicole fell in love with the natural village environment she found in Owere and the village life she saw raw; not the ones she read about in the books. She was a half-cast with a Nigerian father and American mother but looks more American than Nigerian. Besides she followed her mother when they divorced and had never lived in any African soil before.

In any case, some people still believed it was the father's death that devastated him and pardoned the mistakes he made as a prince that he had "always" been, like not knowing the names of his siblings or going to fetch something by himself when he had servants.

Ocheze, his mother, was taken aback somehow about all that may have happened to Ezenobi- real mothers and their children, they know them well. They know the difference even between their very identical twins. She had a misgiving about the returnee, Ezenobi which she couldn't explain. In

The Freeborn Slaves.

her mind, she believed that all was not well with the child of her breast. It was either the kidnappers had put a spell on him to turn his eyes or the *Oyibo* girl he had married charmed him and turned him into something else. Her mind kept telling or suggesting to her that the lad she had under her roof this time around was not the one she had nurtured. However, after some time, even Ocheze got confused and concluded that maybe her son actually misbehaved those initial times because of shock.

Chapter 45.

Ezenobi had acclimatized and become a true prince. With the help of Nicole, he got used to palace etiquette and things were just falling into place. The king's cabinet had been meeting with the *Onowu*- the second in command to the king, at the palace since the Igwe died, but as soon as Ezenobi returned, he joined them. From them, he picked the needed knowledge of what governance was all about.

So many things caught his interest and fancy as he sat among the *Ndi-Ichie*- the palace chiefs. He realized that the success and growth of any society depended on the quality of its leaders and it baffled him why leaders would prefer to see their subjects suffer while they pursued their selfish ends rather than salvage the people from situations where they could. "Why do leaders waste destinies?" he often wondered. It was selfishness to the extent of madness as he had put it.

He became happy that he was among the team that is working to remedy the situation and he vowed to keep his vow to BigChild, Abo, and to The Don. "I shall play my part to the letter," he vowed. He would have to keep sentiments behind him and forget all that he had suffered personally in the past if he hoped to achieve any success. "Personal interests must come second after the general interest," he told himself.

The Freeborn Slaves.

Now, Ezenobi had become the king- Igwe Chinemeze of Owere. He had a way of interacting with the freeborn and the Osu that baffled all others. He had played the game on both sides of the divide and thus it was not difficult for him to blend or mingle with the slaves and freeborn. It was as though the works of the team abroad took time to unfold inside him. He brings ideas that make even him marvel at the embedded wisdom that he sometimes wonders if they actually originated from him. "That's my child," Ocheze his mother acclaimed of him. The eulogies to him now make his queen mother proud that they had sent him abroad.

Though not very grounded in the things of the spirits and spirituality, he had converted and believed it when the Rev. Father had preached love and oneness among neighbors and the need to commune with what the priest had called the Holy Spirit. He usually knelt down and called upon the revered Spirit to help him make wise decisions just as the priest had counseled him. He had a special way of handling things that all and sundry wondered about. He respected everyone's views and gave all the freedom to worship God however they liked. "You can't fight for God because He knows His own," he advised. The faith in oneness returned to the village as all lived and cohabited without qualms, all thanks to the king, Igwe Chinemeze's leadership style. The administration of Owere matters was not as difficult as the ***Ndi-Oha*** had envisaged.

Little drops make the mighty ocean so they say. As such, over time Ezenobi was able to chip in bit by bit suggestions

The Freeborn Slaves.

that would pave the way for his plans. This is the "***Koko-*** the real deal" - the freedom, he continually reminded himself. Even Cassandra was always making him remember the reason she was there- freedom for the Ogbodu people. She had traveled after one year of her stay in the two-in-one village and come back. Her mom couldn't believe it when she saw her daughter Cassandra come back with a little baby girl she called her own daughter even though she was not the biological mother. Something that started like play had turned out into a serious bond. Ezenobi would have married Nicole but she declined for personal reasons. Nevertheless, she pledged her support for the whole "project" as she had referred to it. She had developed an untold liking for the village that even when she was traveling, there was no question or fear as to whether she would come back or not. In fact, she had to force herself to travel so as to confirm to her mom that all was well with her.

Charity begins at home thus Ezenobi made his people see the harm the caste system had done to their generations, the many souls that had died during wars, and all that followed. He made them see the equality of all human beings, how God can use anyone to achieve his purposes, and how the whole world now looked at slavery.

Times have changed and all was to adapt and abide by the new breeze of change blowing all over the village. At a chosen time, the king convoked a general conference whereby he invited some speakers to address his people. He fed them and ensured they were put in a happy mood. The

The Freeborn Slaves.

king, Nicole, and other speakers took turns addressing issues bothering peace, unity, oneness, and the general issues that would benefit the entire village. Before now, Nicole had given a kind of lecture where she first educated the Igwe and his council, and later some prominent youths of Owere village about the inherent harm and danger of the Osu caste system and the possible gains of oneness. Ijeuwa who was back in the village was coopted and made the leader of the women's wing of Igwe Chinemeze's administration and she led them well. She pioneered causes that immensely benefited the womenfolk. Leaders of different clans who were briefed beforehand were also given a chance to air their views during the conference.

"It always boils down to dialogue" BigChild had said.

Igwe Chinemeze played his politics well such that at the conference, many Owere people, including some notable **Ndi-Ichie,** confessed resentment to the divisive caste tradition saying it was obsolete. They said that it bred hate and retrogress, corruption, subjection, and oppression. "All should be given equal opportunity to contribute their talents for the good of all," they said.

During his speech, the king, Igwe Chinemeze asked for forgiveness from the Ogbodu clan on behalf of the Owere clan. He equally enjoined the people of Ogbodu to put behind them whatever ugly experiences they had and allow the new air of peace to blow and their leader accepted on their behalf. Afterward, a peace treaty was signed by the leaders of the different camps. In the new treaty, Igwe

The Freeborn Slaves.

Chinemeze ensured that he restored the sovereignty of the different parts that make up the village. He also ensured that the presence of **Osuimi** Monitors among the other communities was abolished. They were returned to their Owere village. Every part was to own, live, and govern their side of the land and bring returns to the central government which was saddled with the maintenance of the territorial integrity of all including their military protection.

By this time Ohuabunwa had fully got his life back since his brother's return. Even in his previous state of mind, he had refused to partake in the meeting or take the throne saying that since Agu Ngwu the village chief priest had said Ezenobi was still alive, the throne belonged to him. As time went on, he aligned with the wind of change and even changed his name to Nwabunwa meaning that any child is a child; his former name implied that an Osu is no child. It was amazing how smooth the whole thing turned out that even Nicole was vividly happy. Although it was partly the money that drove her to accept the offer, she soon realized the incomparability of the amount with the joy she now shares in liberating and putting smiles on other people's faces. She was glad to have accepted the offer after all. It was as if an eternal kingdom of peace from on high had come upon the entire community.

BigChild and Ezenobi were equally happy each time they talked about how successful their plans had been. Ezenobi led his people with maturity and purpose and above all with

The Freeborn Slaves.

the pulse of his people's hearts. He exuded both in character and appearance what a true African king is all about

....

"I want us to run an open door and an all-inclusive government where all our people would be allowed to make contributions to the decisions we make because it affects them," Ezenobi had begun as he addressed his people a few months into his reign. "We are not going to run our village based on populism, rather I would want us to do what is morally good for all both in the now and in the future, and let posterity be our judge," he said and paused to feel the people's pulse. And truly, many were enthralled by the affection in the tone of his voice as he said 'we', something that his predecessors never said. They had always lorded over them and made them submit to the numerous oaths given them.

"Eeeeh, this is truly the beginning of a new dawn in our land," said one to his friend.

"A king is saying 'we'?" wondered another in a low tone, "***Ezechitoke,*** God we thank you! We will be alive to see and partake in this whole new era,"

Seeing the enthusiasm in their eyes, Ezenobi went on;

"I would have to expose my ignorance in order to enlighten you on my understanding. Let me ask some questions that, maybe, I would still have to try hard to

The Freeborn Slaves.

provide answers to," he went on, "How have division into Ogbodu camp and Owere camp, the classification of one as Osu or as the property of the other, deprivation of the common good to some, disrespect for some humans and their dignities, desecration of the sanctity of human life- in fact, how have all these and the caste system of our land helped us? What progress has it afforded us? What…" he was saying with traces of tears in his eyes.

The chiefs had become sober and sat in absolute silence as they ruminated over the sudden twist of events and the wind of change hovering in the air. Ezenobi had taken all and sundry by storm.

"I will beat my chest gladly, boldly and proudly to say no!" he went on, in a voice that clarified his intent more quickly, "Nooo, they have not helped us in any way, rather, they have only helped to keep our village far behind our compatriots. Why, because we have not allowed all to bring in his or her quotas to move us to where we ought to be. "Generations of our people have come and gone and all these years, we have been given the responsibility to touch lives and make them better… make our lives better and make our land better but we have failed all along… why? Selfishness, greed, ego, self-centeredness, and this must stop for our own good."

We have to wake up and take up our pride of place. We have to allow reason to replace selfish ambitions. We…" he was

The Freeborn Slaves.

saying but many of the chiefs were already clapping their hands spontaneously even to his surprise.

"I would have to finish because what I need is not just the applause, but your cooperation shown through united and committed efforts to make the necessary shift to a better and more fertile ground. We all are one- from Owere or from Ogbodu, we all are descendants of the same man as he had made us and wanted us to be."

"Ichie Chima and all those we are told fought for this freedom would have cherished this day," said one Ichie to another.

"Even in the land of our ancestors," supported the neighbor, "he will be glad to see what our land had finally turned out to be."

From the recommendations of the conference, a committee was constituted comprising all the heads of every kindred, women and youths from both Owere and Ogbodu, and the members of the cabinet. The committee drew up a guide for the progress of the people.

Then at the next meeting with the committee, he informed his them of his intention to dissolve the caste system. It was not as easy as he had expected because change is never easy. A very strong opposition arose against his proposition. Nevertheless, after intense deliberation in a number of meetings, a sizable majority agreed and they outlawed the caste system.

The Freeborn Slaves.

With the treaty signed and the caste outlawed, they went to the '*Onu-Arua*' and reversed all the negative declarations, proclamations, and vows made by their ancestors concerning the Osu practice. They equally reversed all the countless oaths, and agreements they had undertaken both for themselves and their future generations. They equally declared both the words and their consequences null and void and of no effect again.

Before this time, just as he was crowned the Igwe, Ezenobi had married Nwachukwu a pretty damsel only meant for a king, and a kingdom's palace. She was a daughter to one of the former chiefs and the prettiest maiden in the whole land of Owere. In a very big bash, Igwe Chinemeze had crowned her ***Ezenwanyi Nwaolaedo***- Queen Goldenchild. They never knew his intentions then. He was already living the mixture before preaching it.

Traditionally, it was a taboo in fact an abomination for a freeborn to get married to an Osu or for a freeborn to sleep under the same roof with an Osu but now, with the caste gone, some wise men from the Ogbodu clan were made members of the king's cabinet. It was an awesome experience because as time went on, many confessed that most of the good suggestions came from men from the Ogbodu side.

Time has changed. Everyone is free to intermingle, free to associate, very free to marry anyone of his or her choice; no more slaves or freeborn. They shared their common heritage

The Freeborn Slaves.

with equality, equity, and love. Anyone was free to fetch water from the Iyieti Lake or the Iyiocha Rivers without one having precedence to fetch before the other and the people all enjoyed it. "The rivers and the natural resources were all gifts from *Ezechitoke* and should be treated as such," Ezenobi had said to his people, "God was not mistaken when he created us all human and put us together. We have a common destiny to protect." He made them realize what a common destiny they all had. The two-in-one village had become one, and everyone was just happy. They all praised *Ezechitoke* God for coming to their aid through Ezenobi.

"The white men may not be as bad as we judged them after all," some concluded.

"Maybe we judged them harshly before," others said.

"This white man's education is good," they agreed.

"Yes, and we now have to bring back the schools for the benefit of all" the king said.

Chapter 46.

Yes, all these years, many were usually on the king's side in many of his decisions but there were still the irredeemable ones among the *Ndi-Ichie* who all of a sudden did not see anything good in his decisions anymore. They would no longer submit to his banner especially when the council didn't stand to gain instant gratification.

These disgruntled chiefs raised killers among the villagers to undermine every effort by the king and the council to develop the community properly. The hoodlums fomented troubles left, right, and center as they had vowed to fight Ezenobi the king, and his government to a standstill. They were especially miffed by the decision to return the village lands to the rightful owners, and for instituting a period of years after which ownership of the village properties would have to be renewed. They feared that if the whole village became so "one" like that, then they would not possess large shares of the village property as they had possessed all the while. As such, the fertile land of the Ogbodu which they have been enjoying would cease. The soil and farmlands on the Ogbodu side have always been more fertile than those on the Owere side. In fact, that was the major reason the first *Ntisa* crusader returned to the caste system.

Their affront reached its height in the seventh year of Igwe Chinemeze's reign. The infidels joined forces with their enemies to fight their own people.

The Freeborn Slaves.

Igwe Chinemeze had joined forces with the Ogbodu youths when he had a dispute with Igwe Ogwugwu the king of Ogwugwu village and this didn't go down well with the "Irredeemables". The Ogwugwu village had a treaty with the Owere village concerning some choice lands and palm trees. When Igwe Chinemeze studied the treaty, he saw how lopsided its motives were. He immediately saw it was the fallout of the desire to mistreat the Osu of the Ogbodu clan. Owere people had given the property to them as compensation for helping them in the war against Ogbodu.

United with the youths, the king and his cabinet had gone to demand the cancellation of the treaty but the king of Ogwugwu would not play such a ball. Ezenobi had called his bluff and declared the area a returned property of the Owere people. He stationed red-eyed warriors comprising men and women at the village boundaries thereby sealing off the escape routes through which Ogwugwu and other enemies used to come in to molest the Ogbodu women and girls. As a result, they had equally closed their own borders too and this angered those Owere palace chiefs who equally did some escapades with the women of such villages too. They recruited the riff-raffs and made them cause all sorts of trouble. The Owere people passed a decree of **catch and fire** against the irredeemable and their co-riff-raffs and this forced some of them to flee Owere village. Just when they thought they had brought them under their sovereignty, the aggressors went and united with the Ogwugwu village against their own Owere people.

The Freeborn Slaves.

Now, Owere had united with Ogbodu and they presented a stronger front. This was demonstrated the first time they went to demand their land from Igwe Ogwugwu.

"And what would a little boy like you do if I refuse to cancel the treaty? Treaties are not canceled just like that! I have reservations concerning the man seated here as the king," Igwe Ogwugwu had mocked.

"What?" shouted the Owere chiefs and their people.

"What what?" Igwe Ogwugwu retorted, "This man seated here can't possibly be the son of the king, Igwe Anunti."

"You are a joker!" Igwe Chinemeze managed to reply. He had some fears inside. He didn't know whether his enemy had facts. Fetish people have fetish and mystic powers and Igwe Chinemeze knew that.

"I'm not a joker and you know it… usurper!"

"Don't you dare talk to my king in that light!" Akprike the king's bodyguard retorted. He is a boy from Ogbodu. He shouted the loose-mouthed Igwe Ogwugwu down just as he grabbed Ogwugwu's bodyguard who had risen to confront him, and raised him up in the air before yanking him back to his seat.

War broke out between the two villages. BigChild believes he is never to lose in any contest. Although the Ogwugwu

The Freeborn Slaves.

village seemed more like the looser, the outcome was messy. The two sides lost scores of their soldiers.

"Now I need to consult my father!" BigChild had shouted one night during the war hoping to see Abo immediately. He has just lost Ogwube, a famous warrior, and the loss was just too much for him to take.

"No!" BigChild heard right, "You can't consult him any longer. You have been led to the stream and it's your duty to drink or not drink. Or would you rather let him marry a wife for you, and still help with the night duties? You are both men with the balls between your legs."

"Now you have called the bluffs of a dreaded king," BigChild said to Ezenobi courageously afterward, "and you have to maintain it."

"What?!" Ezenobi wondered terrified.

"You have touched the tiger's tail you know," BigChild continued, "and only tigers can get away with it."

Ezenobi remained speechless. He didn't know what to say again. The whole thing had tired him out.

"Yes," BigChild went on, "now that you have called their bluffs, they too would be afraid of you. They would wonder what's behind you because usually spiritually, a bird dancing in the middle of the road has its drummers not far away."

The Freeborn Slaves.

However, it appeared they succeeded in intimidating Igwe Ogwugwu and his people. He demanded a round table talk which was promptly granted with mixed feelings on the Igwe Chinemeze's side. The Owere villagers never knew what he was going through. He wasn't sure of what his enemy knew but he really showed the power of the king. He never betrayed his emotions. Too, Igwe Ogwugwu would not just succumb to such cheap pressure. He has to fight on.

…………………………………………………………………..

"What papers?" Igwe Chinemeze asked, confusion and terror written all over him.

"Yes, what papers?" Igwe Ogwugwu returned mockingly, "You are asking me? Hahahahaaaa!"

"We will get it!" BigChild cut in.

"Get it then!" Igwe Ogwugwu replied and his happiness knew no bounds as he made signs to indicate that his visitors had overstayed their welcome. He now believes he has cause to believe that the man sitting before him didn't know a thing concerning the treaty he sought to cancel otherwise they wouldn't have gone to war in the first place. He was only waiting to confirm his suspicion before invading Owere to take back the returned pieces of land.

Every third year, they changed the symbol of the treaty just to remind themselves that the land and the properties still belonged to Owere. Now, Igwe Chinemeze had been on the

The Freeborn Slaves.

throne for more than nine years and he never said anything about it. The irredeemable ***Ndi-Ichie*** knew this but they weren't sure of what was going on. Too, what really baffled Igwe Ogwugwu was the seeming inability of Ezenobi to even recognize his supposed friend and colleague- the heir to the Ogwugwu throne.

At the last exchange of symbols, they had replaced the papers with their respective seals engraved on half a golden crown. Their slogan was always a question and answer for instance running thus; "Where are the papers?" and the answer would be, "No more papers, I need my royal seal on the crown." This was all Igwe Ogwugwu had expected from his guest.

Ezenobi had been part and parcel of the previous treaties and thus shouldn't be a novice at all. It was Ezenobi's probable forgetfulness of the Igwe Ogwugwu's son's name that had triggered his suspicions. They had met a couple of times since his becoming the king of Owere village, but he never called the Ogwugwu heir by name or showed any sign of knowing him before.

"Hey, Egwuoma," Ezenobi- the Igwe Chinemeze had suddenly and unconsciously called as they stood to go from the round table talk. As soon as he called that name, something exploded inside him. He recalled all at once everything that Ezenobi had said under hypnosis, concerning a certain Egwuoma. Now, the stories all came rushing back into his memory.

The Freeborn Slaves.

Igwe Ogwugwu was shocked and taken aback and off-guard. He became instantly cold and confused. He wondered whether Igwe Chinemeze had been purposely tricking him and playing the ignorant. The two kings were individually lost in the confusion in their minds. Each had noticed the confusion in the other's face but couldn't place what it was they were both confused about. Their subjects who had equally noticed their confusion simply looked on confused too.

"I told you it may be the effect of the kidnap and trauma or just sheer trick." Egwuoma blamed his father later on.

"You may be right, my son" Igwe Ogwugwu agreed but still half-heartedly. "

....

"What shall we do?" Ezenobi enquired from BigChild in a frustrated voice. They are now alone like always whenever they want to discuss a secret matter.

"Don't panic," BigChild began, "just cool down so you can think straight."

"This one is not about thinking straight o, I need help!" Ezenobi yelled throwing his hands up and down in frustration and resignation.

"So what do we do?" BigChild asked.

The Freeborn Slaves.

"You are asking me?" Ezenobi fired back, "I need you to think for me," he cried.

"Think for you?" BigChild wondered, "Not me."

As they quarreled and squabbled, they realized how helpful Abo would have been but he had bailed out since long time ago and no one seemed to know where he had gone to. As Ezenobi shut his eyes in deep thought, he sank deeper into confusion. Funny and scary thoughts flooded his mind in their millions. He imagined how disgraceful and shameful it would be when the people found out the truth about him. The disgrace and the eventual shameful death would just be too much and he would never allow himself to experience such. How would he convince anyone that he did not kill Ezenobi or exonerate himself from Igwe Anunti's death?

"Abo would not come now to carry the prey of his trap," Ezenobi screamed, "He led us into this!" he opened his eyes as if he wanted to behold Abo just then.

"But we have been enjoying all the accolades and..." BigChild chipped in comically but Ezenobi was not in the mood. BigChild now lives in the Pa Lui The Don's mansion which on his instruction, had been rebuilt claiming it to be a tribute to the late hero. He had become the pseudo-traditional prime minister.

"Hey, I knew it!" Ezenobi continued, "This Abo is always bad news. He has led us, in fact, he had tricked me again into the middle of the stream... only to forsake me

The Freeborn Slaves.

right there. Now what papers is that grabber talking about?" he cried.

"Why saying you?" BigChild hollered, "Say 'we'! We are together in this!" BigChild harshly reassured him. He had always displayed a commitment to this struggle that baffled and thrilled Ezenobi. Though BigChild acts the boss and goes to all extents to make Ezenobi realize that he calls the shots, they have moved on well without troubles. "Cool down," Bigchild said calmly now, "Whatever begins ends, just as whatever is hot must surely become cold. Whatever goes up must come down someday. I have heard and I believe too in the truthfulness that the fire given to a son by his father would not burn him."

Ezenobi has become calm now. Like a sweet lullaby, the words from BigChild's lips simply suited him in a way he could not explain.

"Yes, I believe you!" Ezenobi cheered, "We are together in this, BigChild. Besides, this fire, this power, this authority, and the audacity given to me cannot consume me. It was given to me in the land of the spirits; the land where stars and warriors are made. Yes, this fire cannot be extinguished in the land of mortals. I have come, I can see, and surely, I'm determined to conquer," he finished reassuringly calmly.

"Yes!" Abo exclaimed as he came through the door, "That's the man! The brilliant valiant man of valor! Fearfully brave like the lion, he runs and turns sharply to attack its attacker. Be strong and think and in the long run, your praise won't be wrong on the people's tongues."

"Where have you been?!" Igwe Chinemeze hollered and rushed towards Abo. Then he stopped abruptly and turned back as Abo had retreated sharply and exited through the same door he was coming from. As the two, BigChild and Ezenobi, wondered in their confusion, an echo reverberated, and "Search your house" was heard within the echo.

"Search the house?" Ezenobi wondered.

They searched the entire house but found nothing to their benefit. The whole palace and its environs were always swept clean so they didn't know what they were required to do. However, they did as they heard and that was that.

Just then, Kamsiyo, a ten-year-old girl from the Ogbodu side, who was living with them in the palace came running to Igwe Chinemeze. Now in Kamsiyo's hand was half a golden crown she claimed was given to her by a stranger standing at the palace gate.

"The man said you should say this," Kamsi had begun, "Whenever you hear "where's the papers, you are to answer, "No more papers, I need my royal seal on the crown."

"Where is the man?" BigChild and Ezenobi asked simultaneously,

The Freeborn Slaves.

"Right at the gate," she replied.

"Where?" they queried hurriedly.

"At the gate under the cocoa-nut tree where he dug up this," the little girl reported handing the half crown to Igwe Chinemeze.

They both started towards the gate and suddenly Kamsiyo was nowhere to be found. They wondered what was happening and suddenly they saw her playing the "*Akwua*" game with her friends and some other children under the mango tree down the compound. Her friends and all claimed Kamsiyo had sat there all along and never left there nor brought any golden crown to the "*Obi*"- the palace's sitting room. Ezenobi and BigChild looked and beheld a man walking far down the footpaths and concluded it ought to be Abo.

They took their own half of a golden crown and it was with mixed feeling that Igwe Ogwugwu accepted it. He still had a misgiving about Igwe Chinemeze that he couldn't explain.

"This matter still has to be investigated!" Igwe Ogwugwu had sneered as he bade them farewell but the visitors never replied to it. Only BigChild and Igwe Chinemeze knew what Igwe Ogwugwu and his rants meant. Others simply saw him as an angry bad looser grumbling after a big loss. However, the treaty was canceled and that was that. Igwe Chinemeze had won or so he thought and it was to the admiration of his subjects.

The Freeborn Slaves.

The Freeborn Slaves.

Chapter 47.

Everybody was just happy and they all knew and acknowledged it. Attama Ngwu the priest of Ngwu forest, though nearly a century old now still remembered the prophecy he was given, that when the kidnapped Igwe resurfaced, the whole villagers were happy. He only got confused when he remembered that in his vision, he had seen the crown leave and elude the entire Owere village unto an unknown head of an unknown face. But here he was; he knew this Igwe Ezenobi and this confused him. The few people he had told about it agreed with him that the village had recorded unprecedented progress since the return of Igwe Chinemeze.

"But don't we all know Ezenobi?" argued Chukwude who has become an elder too as he looked at the Ngwu priest one evening under the *"Uvuru"* tree where they usually enjoyed their evenings.

"Prophecies don't always come straight," the priest consoled both himself and Chukwude.

"Yes, prophecies don't always come straight," they all agreed even though Chikwude still had some reservations, "maybe he was actually from another village but we didn't know." he murmured while the priest cast him a sneering look and let the sleeping dog lie.

The Freeborn Slaves.

The Freeborn Slaves.

Chapter 48.

Many years had passed, and even with the ups and downs, many positive changes had been recorded. The Orie market had expanded tremendously. The schools which the predecessors expelled were returned and the place of excellent knowledge was extolled. Cathedrals and mosques were not left out either. The people who had left the village since the fight of the ancestors began to return again. The attendant darkness over the land by the acts of the previous kings was wearing away and giving way to a bright new dawn. He had set his people's future on the pedestal of progress and development. Everywhere just kept opening up and the people couldn't but thank *Ezechitoke* for their new king. The people all lived in harmony and happiness. It has become like it used to be as they heard about the good old days of their ancestor, Owere. Everyone loved their land where those born in the East or West, bought in the East, or sold in the West lived freely and felt safe and secure. There was no more distinction between those who could watch the masquerades perform and those who could not. Everyone's eyes have become sacred and good enough to watch all the masquerades except those forbidden to women.

The king Igwe Chinemeze had returned the lands of the Owere, the Umuokpu, the Ogbodu, and all others to their rightful owners. It was then instituted that every seventh year, the villagers would return the village lands and other properties to their family heads who would then return them to the royal council. The properties would then be reassigned

The Freeborn Slaves.

to new owners. This was to ensure that overriding ambitions do not arise in people's hearts and minds. The people would have it in their minds that it was only a matter of time before whatever village property they possessed would return to the people. They all took appropriate care of the properties since one never knew which property would be assigned to him. and the status quo may be maintained. He ensured that all his subjects lived in peace and security throughout his kingdom.

He equally made them rethink their agricultural way of life which they were unknowingly but gradually abandoning owing to the ballooning and bourgeoning businesses in their Orie market.

On the day of his seventeenth anniversary on the throne, the king prepared a very big bash for his subjects, the kind that had never been seen. He had always given them an "*Ohabiarie*" kind of celebration whereby everyone was invited to come and eat, but this time, even the people who cooked were contracted from the city. The Owere village had become friends with many neighboring villages and their kings were equally invited to join in the rejoicing too. Many traditional dances especially the famous Ikorodo, Adabara, and Atiliogwu dance groups were in attendance to liven up the occasion. BigChild and even members of the organizing committee were surprised at the enormous money and energy put out for this particular *Ofalla* celebration. It was not a jubilee, so they all wondered why all the extras. Hard as BigChild tried, Igwe the king refused to divulge his intentions and it baffled him. BigChild believes he calls the

The Freeborn Slaves.

shots but the king, Igwe Chinemeze sees it differently. He believes the inspiration for the smooth running of his kingdom and even his elongated stay in power was his devotion to the revered Spirit.

On the highly anticipated day, everybody had assembled at the village square- the Obodo Owere as usual. Their anniversaries had never been marked with violence since the installation of Ezenobi, the Igwe Chinemeze of Owere village, so the people wondered why he had to invite the police from the city, but he explained it away saying that the many traditional rulers from other villages needed adequate security. He however assured everyone of their safety.

"*Ndi be anyi, kwen o!*" the king, Igwe Chinemeze greeted the villagers after they had all enjoyed themselves to a large extent.

"*Yaa!*" they replied.

"*Ndi-Ichie, kwenu o,*" he greeted

"*Yaa!*"

"Elders of Owere, *kwenu o!*"

"*Yaa!*"

"*Ndi obia anyi, kwenu o*" he greeted the visitors

The Freeborn Slaves.

"*Yaa*!" they thundered. They were always happy to respond each time he greeted them. They were all happy with him or at least the majority was.

"*Ala Owere kwenu o!*"

"*Yaa!*"

"*Umu Owere, kwezuenu ooo!*"

"*Yaaa!*" they heartily chorused in utter happiness.

"We thank *Ezechitoke* for today," he went on, "A day like today is always sweet and memorable. It doesn't come always."

"Yes ooooo!" the villagers agreed.

"It is now seven and seven and three years since I assumed the throne left to me by fate."

"By fate?" some people wondered, "Oh yes by fate," they now remembered but some still continued to process the statement even without knowing why. "And we have been happy ever since like never before," they still agreed all the same.

"We have seen the benefits of living in oneness and harmony, in brotherliness, in love, and above all in peace of equality," Igwe the king went on. "*Ife a di ka nwanne-* there's nothing as sweet as being brothers to each other."

"Igweeeeeeee!" they cheered him.

The Freeborn Slaves.

"Thanks be to God, '*Ezechitoke eme o*'" he went on.

"Yes o, my king, Igweeee," supported another, "***Chukwu Abiama eme*** - God has done it."

"Within such a short time, we have recorded success and progress beyond measure in all ramifications. We have prospered together because we learned to give everyone and every part its needed freedom. We gave the needed support to one another and everyone got a fair share of the general resources. We have grown in numbers and so have our strength increased. While not looking down on our guests and neighbors, we dare say that we now have the most insurmountable and impregnable army in all the nearest horizons. We have seen the strength of our unity in diversity. Our people are respected everywhere because we have learned to remain one and be one another's keepers. We have fought only a few wars since our coming on board all because our enemies fear our strength of unity. It's all because we decided to live together as one in mutual respect and dignity of all. Division will always divide and unity will always unite, and so I must thank the royal cabinet members the ***Ndi-Ichie*** and elders of this land, and indeed every son and daughter of this great land who chose to follow us on a common vision. Owere is one people and one we shall remain!"

"***Iseee!***" they all chorused in consonance with the prayer. "It shall continue."

The Freeborn Slaves.

"*Iseee*!" Igwe joined in agreement with their prayer. "My joy knows no bounds today as I speak to you, and how I wish that my heart could be opened to let all see the fullness of joy in it."

Everywhere had become calm while he spoke.

"I greet you all and thank you all for the immense support you have given me. I couldn't have done it all alone. I never knew I could lead nor be adjudged a good one at that. Even many people wouldn't have believed it. This tells me that something good can come from anyone and that there is actually no reason why we should fight one another. There is no reason for us to be divided when we are created to be brothers and sisters born with equal opportunities and good gifts from God for the good of all. Thank you all for your support and…"

"You even deserve more than that," some said and sincerely too.

"I urge you to give even greater support to whoever you shall choose to be your next king the Igwe because…" he glanced looking somewhat startled. Maybe it was his mind playing tricks on him. It couldn't have been the '*Oja Aya*'- war flute that he heard. Some others equally felt or thought they heard the sound too.

"What is he saying?" many wondered and murmured among themselves, "This is beyond belief! Is he wishing himself death? How could he say such thing? Talking about

The Freeborn Slaves.

the next Igwe when he is still alive is very unusual. And I don't even know if I heard a sound just now"

"It's really strange o, is he bringing outside warriors to kill everyone?" queried one Ichie- palace chief.

"Is anyone after his throne?" asked another, "Let him continue on the throne. And besides, he has sons Chinwoke and Chijindu."

"Even her daughters Obinne and Udechi are better off on the throne than most men."

"Listen" he went on, "I'm not wishing myself death, I know what I am saying."

"I doubt it, Ezenobi, my son!" interjected Ocheze his mother, and then **Ezenwanyi** Nwaolaedo his queen both rising from their seats and moving closer to him. "How could you be wishing yourself such evil?" they queried him

"I am not wishing myself death, but it may be inevitable today," he said.

Before he could finish the statement, Ocheze had collapsed. To the surprise of many, as they battled to save his "mother", and even as his Queen and wife Ezenwanyi Nwaolaedo was trying to stop him, Igwe Chinemeze the king went on with his speech. Not even the wailing of some of his children and friends could deter him. He only allowed the trepidation to die down a little bit before he went on.

The Freeborn Slaves.

"Today is a memorable day as I said earlier, and I want to make it even more memorable."

"Emeodi?" called Nnabike, "I want to go feed my goats," he said fearfully and sarcastically as he dusted his bum and arose immediately to leave.

"I, too," answered Emeodi and they left in fear. Then they suddenly and instantly became stiffly scared of the uniformed men around, and as such they retreated and sat down.

"Nothing will happen to anybody here I assure you," Igwe promised again. "Just listen to what I have to say. It is for the benefit of the entire Owere village... It is the story of when and how I disappeared and reappeared."

"We have heard all that before now," the crowd roared.

"This is the most interesting part of the story that nobody had ever told anybody before," he informed them. "You all say that I am a good king... your Igwe... and that my period on the throne had brought tremendous progress and unification. Now," he pursed and cleared his throat, "it is a big lesson for us all because the truth shall shake and break us and then make us and teach us all some truths about life," Igwe was crying this time as he said these.

"Some people's blood was shed in the struggle for the freedom, unity, prosperity and peace we all enjoy now.

The Freeborn Slaves.

Those were the hero's past; some we have honored but it will be impossible to honor all the visionary people of this great land; indigenes and settlers whose ambitions of great Owere land were cut short. They had the interest of all of us in their hearts but were denied the opportunity to express or actualize them simply because of where they were born. Heads rolled and blood flowed all over the place for the entirety of the people to be free as God had intended for them,".

"I respect and adore all those whose blood was shed in the struggle to take us all back to our common and individual destinies. May they have peace and eternal rest with the Almighty and with our ancestors."

Many would have said '*Iseee*' to support his prayers for the deceased but they were too afraid and confused and lost in thought to even hear him properly. So many would have gone back home if not for the uniformed policemen around. They didn't trust the promise of 'no harm to anybody' by the Igwe.

"Some people took it upon themselves," he went on, "and sacrificed generations and fortunes to secure it. What can we do for these people other than to ensure that we sustain the gains that we now see and profess with our own lips? These had been their dreams. These had been their visions and ambitions. They saw what others couldn't see and now even though they are no longer alive physically to enjoy the result of their visions, we can make them do so by

The Freeborn Slaves.

living continually on this bright side of light shining gloriously over our land." Thus, I am not trying to rekindle old wounds and memories but I must give yet again honor to whom it's due and as well state that good things can come from anybody irrespective of where he is from. Man has not been given the power to choose where to be born. More importantly, no particular people were born to rule and the others were born to follow. And as it seems, **Ezechitoke** uses the weak to shame those who think they are wise or strong. Let's build bridges rather than gullies."

"These sermons are rather heading to something we may never have anticipated," said one woman.

"This food we ate today, eh?" replied her neighbor, "It's about to bring our legs out to the roads."

"I feel like vomiting it out," said her friend. "I wouldn't have come."

"Even me. it was my husband that made me come o," the woman shifted blame.

"No one chose for himself or herself where to be born," Igwe maintained, "I must thank the family of Dr. Erics who accepted that the mission of our ancestor would be fulfilled."

"Ours had been a hard lesson learned the hard way," Chukwude chipped in as he suited Oge, his daughter, who kept calling for her mother.

The Freeborn Slaves.

"To cut a long story short," Igwe went on, tears in his radiant eyes, "I am Achuzie Ogbodo and not Ezenobi as I have claimed all these years."

"What?!" many exclaimed in total bewilderment, "What did he just say?" they kept wondering, shouting and covering their eyes and ears from the hard news that just hit them. They couldn't believe they heard right.

Attama Ngwu recalled the vision he saw earlier, and he looked at Chukwude, and the few people he had told about it.

"You doubter!" he sneered at Chukwude.

"I won't explain how it happened," Igwe began, "but just like all the compatriots, we mortgaged our lives as a ransom for our collective freedom, peace, and unity. I therefore leave you and posterity to be the judge of whether what we did in the struggle was right or wrong as I submit myself to the appropriate authority."

Just then the sound of the '*Oja Aya*' and the marching feet of warriors became nearer and clearer. This time, even Igwe Chinemeze the king was startled and it showed. He had his guards and warriors stationed as always at the various *Ama* Owere, but one cannot always be too sure. But if anything was amiss, he expected the village *Ohuzo* the seer, who always climbed the Lebeuwa Mountain to have run here to inform him. At the top of Lebeuwa Mountain, *Ohuzo* was able to see all the roads and entrances into Owere village.

The Freeborn Slaves.

Many now knew the sound they had heard and equally knew there was a snake in the rafters. Some dared to run away from the arena "before someone's property turns to another's" as they had put it in defiance of their fear of the police.

On BigChild's insistence, Achuzie had overstayed his tenure by many years and this had infuriated Abo. Since the position of an Igwe- the king was a political one and not the traditional *Eze* kingship which used to be hereditary, Achuzie as the king Igwe Chinemeze was to reign for ten years and then institute a plan whereby the people chose who would become their king through election thereby ending the monarch system they practiced. However, BigChild had reneged on the agreement saying that they had performed creditably well and should be commended rather than being "chased out" as he had put it. "Power is sweet," he always said and this only furthered the anger Abo already had. He no longer appeared to them, but they were aware of the agreement all the same. Even when he (BigChild) advised Achuzie to order the rebuilding of the ancient ruins of The Don Lui's mansion and the Achuzies', a voice had interjected. None was to be compensated specially or specifically since they all had suffered in their own different ways. They knew how brisk, direct, and clear the voice was then to mess with it, but still, BigChild had to make Achuzie do it somehow. Even the Anyaoha didn't like that, especially when after rebuilding it, BigChild had gone to occupy it. Then Abo went into action again.

The Freeborn Slaves.

"Probe further into that Owere matter," a voice had said to Igwe Ogwugwu, "There are things you are not clear about."

The Igwe Ogwugwu was startled. He never heard a voice so strange and clear like that before. He was still thinking about it when it came the second time harder- almost in a nagging manner.

"Probe further," it had said, "Igwe Chinemeze is a usurper and he has incurred the wrath of those whose stooge he is." He couldn't believe it. A voice speaking so clearly from the blues- it's impossible. Yes, he had heard the voices of the spirits in his shrines but never this clear. Now, "a stooge?" he wondered, "By who?" questions flooded his mind and he soon realized the urgency of the need to 'probe further' as the voice had demanded. It wasn't too hard for him though.

As the village had become one again, after they had rebuilt the ancient ruins of The Don's mansion, and even after Casandra-Nicole had gone home, BigChild had reasoned that it would be wise to inform the Anyaoha's who he truly was but the king Igwe Chinemeze refused. The Anyaoha's people had become apprehensive that while other people's properties were being returned to them, theirs was rebuilt and given to a stranger- "Maybe to still keep us in check," they had complained. With the passage of years, the pestering and nagging had become almost strangling and BigChild had to let the cat out of the bag to Mazi Ifesi,

The Freeborn Slaves.

Anyaoha's eldest son, that he was Lui's son though he begged him that since they were one family, they should keep it a secret. All these were to the chagrin and distaste of Igwe Chinemeze the king.

"Everyone knows that our family had been chosen to liberate this land" BigChild had bragged one evening, "Now I stand in for my fathers and I call the shots in this village. Even the king's decisions and actions are all under my scrutiny". Sadly, that was about the same time the news hunters came.

The Ogwugwu's informants and foot soldiers had to search and scratch for the secret. The Anyaohas had friends too to whom they had related the revelation though in confidence too. Thus a handful of people already knew about it and tried very hard to protect their little secret as much as they could but maybe it wasn't enough.

Now, Igwe Ogwugwu knew the truth, and to compound the whole mess, he heard that Igwe Chinemeze was hosting the mother of all *Ofalla* festivals, and yet he was not invited. It so infuriated him such that like death, he chose to kill Igwe Chinemeze on a day he thought life was sweetest. First, Igwe Ogwugwu sent his great Dibia Omeribe to go and curse the land of Owere. After the great Omeribe and his lieutenants had gone as commanded, he knew in his mind that his charms did not answer as he called, but he dared not tell Igwe Ogwugwu about such a failure. And so he and his lieutenants had joined Igwe Ogwugwu to organize the warriors and

The Freeborn Slaves.

station them at the Umugwam Hills. As he heard the sound of the peoples' voices as they applauded their king, he thought that that was the right time to strike, and thus he let out the sound of the '*Oja Aya*'.

No one can explain how it happened but the warriors and guards placed at the Umugwam entrance to Owere all fell asleep including the ***Ohuzo*** who was stationed at the Lebeuwa mountains. The other warriors and guards stationed at the other roads and entrances to Owere heard the sound of the ***Oja-Aya*** but as they did not hear a response or wakeup call from their own colleague- the ***Ohuzo***, they thought maybe it was in another village.

Now, one of Igwe Ogwugwu's insider informants had run up to inform him that Igwe Chinemeze was making his anniversary speech, and without even knowing what the speech was all about, he had decided to come down and 'disgrace him out of the throne'. He equally informed him that the road was clear as no guards were on the way. At this information, Igwe Ogwugwu nodded at his dibia the Great Omeribe with a "thank you" look on his face.

Before Achuzie finished his statement, BigChild had stepped forward to stand beside his compatriot. It stung him like the bee but he soon realized where his "scrutinizing of the Igwe's actions and decisions" had landed them. The mystic Abo was nowhere to be found, but BigChild had quickly realized too how true his statement about his inclination to rule had been, and he realized what the mystic meant when he had said, "Oughtn't you to remember to

The Freeborn Slaves.

know when to quit?" They have come to see him as probably the spirit of their ancestor, Owere, who had appeared in human form to accomplish the mission.

Now, the king's confession and revelation had rippled out confusion and division. Some felt that what Achuzie and compatriots did had been in the interest of all and thus should be applauded rather than condemned, while some others- the jungle-minded ones felt they ought to face the consequence of their action. Yet there were those who sat on the fence like the confusing *Usu*- the bat; the only flying mammal. People switched camps; some accused them of murder and usurpation while many others were already protesting that the police were not going to arrest their king the Igwe.

Now, the Ogwugwu village was coming to invade them hoping that the Owere people would support them when they realized who their king had been all along, but now many of the Owere people were already on their king's side and were going to fight on his side.

With the final statement, Achuzie submitted himself and his friend to the police whom he himself had invited. This was before the Igwe Ogwugwu, and his mission unfolded. His Queen Ezenwanyi Nwaolaedo and children joined them. The police soon realized what a double-duty call they had. Just then, the Owere guards and warriors had closed in on the arena and surrounded all. Hard as the Police tried, they could not arrest Achuzie, his cohorts, and his supporters. With the help of the Owere guards and warriors, the Police arrested

The Freeborn Slaves.

and went away with the invaders- Igwe Ogwugwu and his fellow coup plotters.

As they were going away, many saw a young oldie having a field day laughing at the arrested invaders. None knew him except BigChild and Achuzie.

Made in the USA
Columbia, SC
27 January 2025